I0566043

The Purebred and the Mutt

A Romantic Comedy

By

USA Today Bestselling Author

Dani Haviland

Copyright

Copyright © 2021

Dani Haviland and Chill Out! Books

All Rights Reserved

ISBN 978-1-950592-38-8

Names, places, characters, and incidents are the product of the author's imagination or used fictitiously for the reader's entertainment. Any resemblance to persons living, dead, or fictional, events, business establishments, or locales, is entirely coincidental. No part of this book may be used or reproduced in any manner without written permission from the author except for brief quotations in reviews or critical articles.

(Cover by Dani Haviland)

Book Description

Cultures clash when a British celebrity and a proud but poor American wind up under the same roof in Forever, Montana. A stowaway skunk and crazed fan add to the challenges of the two people who have been single for too long.

Enjoy this stand-alone romantic comedy but don't threaten the skunk! He's armed!

Dedication

A big THANK YOU to those great guys of Amazon Prime's THE GRAND TOUR®, the inspirations for my *Around the World in Eighty Cars* series. I've always loved cars, trucks, and motorcycles and usually incorporate at least one into my stories. Well, at least the tales that take place in the 20th and 21st centuries…

Chapter 1

Late Summer
East Mesa, Arizona

Item: AROUND THE WORLD IN 80 CARS has come to Arizona! Come join the fun and watch as your favorite race car drivers and reality TV stars William Gagnant, Morris Donaldson, and Ben Zachary resurrect Mesa Verde Speedway for one more race! Now known as the Mesa Verde Park and Swap, the circuit track was the hot spot for race car enthusiasts from the 60's to late 80's. Put on your time travel gear and break out your love beads and sandals, because this Saturday night, vintage 60's muscle cars are getting another shot at track records.

***

"And here we are folks," Morris boomed over the roar of the track, "William has decided to show off his classic nineteen sixty-four and a half Mustang today. Ben, what do you think of his choice?"

The shortest member of the famed car enthusiast television program looked at the track before speaking. "I think it's mostly nostalgia. Performance-wise, there were better options in the 60s. Not a surprise, William opted for the Power Team combination upgrade on this car and went with the Equa-Lock limited-slip differential, the 289 cubic inch engine, and four-speed manual transmission. To put it simply, he wanted to experience the vehicle as it was available to race enthusiasts in early 1965."

Ben paused for a moment, watching the baby-powder blue Mustang lose control. "The version William is in today was meant for straightaway tracks, quarter-mile drag racing, or – as the Americans say – cruising Main. It's a spoiled young man's car that has become a mid-

1

life crisis fixation for men of today.

"The body style was very posh at the time. Revving the engine with its dual exhaust created throaty, macho growls. Great for a showy ride to the pub, it was also a family man's car, with room in the back seat to take children to the ice cream parlor. All in all, it was a show piece, meant to impress ladies from four to forty."

"Only for show?" Morris asked. "Come on now. Give it a little credit, Ben. It had to have some redeeming value to still be in production."

"That came later," Ben said, "when Mr. Shelby came into the game and added more power to the package. This one – from the inaugural year – would go aught to sixty in just over eight seconds. That's with the 289 V-8, too. That might possibly win drag races against little old ladies in electric wheelchairs or Honda Civics. The car was meant to be driven on straight roads or gentle curves, not racing on roundy-round tracks like the one William is on now."

Both men watched William falter as the rear end of his Mustang lost traction once again, nearly spinning out. "I think he may have been a little bold there, Ben. That track is crumbly, and those six and a half by fourteen-inch tires aren't much bigger than the fat boys on a Schwinn ten-speed bicycle."

"Yes, and a Schwinn has six more gears to use. That engine has got to be screaming, turning at eight grand. I don't know if that little radiator can keep up. There was a reason why so many modifications were made…

Screech! Crash! Bang! Thunk-thunk-thunk!

William had totally lost control and spun out. His powder-blue baby flipped over and over again – at least six times – and landed driver's door down, the wheels spinning uselessly toward the grandstand.

Ben froze, too stunned to speak. He turned to Morris, slack-jawed and ashen.

The big man saw his cohort's shock and took the lead. "There's nothing we can do from here, folks, but pray that William is unhurt. He may be in a 1964 vehicle, but it *was* retrofitted with a rollbar and reinforced doors. Plus, he's wearing the latest state of the art crash gear. Helmet, fire-retardant suit… Oh, my Lord. Cut, cut!"

Morris turned to the cameraman. "That was a first I never wanted to see, Kodak. Where's Joe?"

"Joe the producer?" When he saw Morris's scowl of, 'Of course, you idiot!' Kodak nodded to the fracas below. "He was watching from the pit. He went down ten minutes ago to beg William one more time not to go out on that piece of shit track."

"Well, let's hope we'll be buying get well soon, not sympathy cards," Ben said.

Morris shook his head. "There's no one in William's life to get a sympathy card for, and he'd just throw a get well card in the trash. Whether he likes it or not, William may have to retire to that wild horse ranch in Montana, after all."

Ben grimaced. "That's a whole hell of a lot better than being buried there."

"Hey, look!" Kodak said, pointing. "He's waving! William's okay!"

Still strapped in, William waved through the busted-out windshield frame to let the crew know he was alive, then slumped over the steering wheel in agony. The pain was unbearable. Unconsciousness – or even death – would be better than the pain he felt right now. He sniffed, smelled gasoline, and was hit with a spurt of adrenaline.

Pushing through the pain, he elbowed his way out through the remaining bits of broken windshield glass. He crawled clear of the vehicle then arose, head slumped forward as if asleep. He stumbled ten feet further, then collapsed at the feet of his pit crew.

Kaboom!

***

"Hey, mate," Morris said softly from the side of the hospital bed. "That was a close one. Only one shake of a lamb's tail to spare that time."

"I'm not dead then?" William asked hoarsely. "Because it sure feels like I am."

"Nah," Ben said. "If you were dead, you wouldn't feel any pain. You might get a few sniffles and sneezes from the feathers on your angel wings, though."

William started to laugh at the lame joke but was brought up short by the pain. "Who…who did it?"

"Did what?" Morris asked.

"Saved me."

"Actually, no one claimed credit," Ben said. "It seems you had a supernatural being in there or something."

"Bull."

"No, mate. You had a bit of a Shadrack, Meshack, and Abednego moment there. They even recorded it. You could actually see the smoke move away as the supernatural entity pulled your passed-out body clear."

"Hmph." *Another one of his co-workers' jokes. He wasn't in any shape to argue, though. That would take too much energy.* "Water."

"Say please," Ben chided. "No, I'm just teasing you. The nurse said only ice chips until the doctor sees you. They want to make sure your stomach is empty. I guess you're getting a little hardware installed in your collar bone to go along with your duct-taped ribs."

Morris fed William a spoonful of cracked ice. "Sorry, but they wouldn't let me give you a splash of Scotch to help this go down…"

William started to laugh then groaned in pain. "Don't make me laugh. Please."

"Sorry. You know how it is. We can't help it. It's either make a joke out of it or cry at how close it was." Morris took the spoon back. "Honestly, though, Ben, Kodak, Joe – shoot, the whole crew – all of us thought you were a goner. You were there, stepping away from the car – barely clear of it – then *Boom*!"

Ben picked up the story. "Yes, and next thing we know, you were at the edge of the fiery furnace, dropping to the ground as if someone had just let go of you. Oh, and I hope your leg is okay. The paramedic thought it was broken, but when they brought you in and x-rayed it, they saw it was simply sideways. Well, not simply. It was twisted out of joint. A hefty tug and quick turn and they had it pointed in the right direction again. They said it would be sore for a few weeks, but no permanent damage."

"And…" Morris took a deep breath and grinned, ready to expound on the dramatic and extraordinary part of the story. "The doctor said there was no way you could have walked on that leg. You experienced a miracle, buddy. A class one, 'ooh-wee-ooh' miracle."

"Or 'ooh-wee-ooh' aliens," Ben added. "But just to be on the safe side…" He looked up towards heaven and said, "Thanks, Sir. We'll claim the miracle."

"Oh, and Joe said we're not going to show that footage. As always, anyone who came to see the race had to sign papers that they wouldn't video the event, so hopefully we're safe there."

"Wait, wait. Miracle?" William asked, ignoring the last remark.

Ben looked up at his tall cohort. "I think he's still a little loopy."

"Yes, they did put him on a morphine drip."

"All right, men," the broad-shouldered male nurse said. "It's time for you two to leave and for William to get a little titanium reinforcement installed in that shoulder."

The three co-stars shared good-byes and good lucks then the two turned to leave. The nurse escorted them into the hallway. "By the way, I watch your show all the time, mates. When are we going to see this episode?"

Morris and Ben both shook their heads. Morris said, "It's up to two people: the producer and William. I doubt either one will allow it."

"Why not? He came out alive, right?"

"It's not always about survival of the body," Ben said.

"Oh, yeah," the nurse said. "I guess that would cause a bit of post-traumatic stress for William. You're right. Best to keep that locked up in the film vault. Besides, rumor is, there were aliens involved in his rescue. The media would go nuts with that and conspiracy theories and…"

"Come on, Ben," Morris said, his hand on his teammate's

shoulder, leading him away from another obsessed fan. "Let's get gone and see if we can give Joe a heads up on damage control. Aliens? Hmm. It seems we weren't the only ones who saw what happened. He might have to release the video just to keep the rumor mill starved."

***

"Was I dreaming?" William asked Joe.

"Probably," his show's producer said. "Although, I don't know if you dream when under anesthesia. You were in surgery for five, almost six hours."

"What? Did they decide to give me a bigger dick, too?"

"Nah, they figured since you were single, it was big enough to make one person happy – you."

William started to laugh, then remembered it would hurt and paused. He gave a forced chuckle and realized he was pretty much pain-free. "Well, how about that? They fixed me good." He laughed heartily. "Real good."

"Take it easy there, pal. You're still under the influence of some mighty powerful drugs. The intravenous kind. When those wear off, you'll be given pills. They're pretty stringent on how many, so you might want to investigate some alternative means of pain management."

"You mean like whisky?" William asked with a laugh, giddy at his new, comfortable arrangement.

"No, like meditation, ice, a bit of Ibuprofen…"

"Maker's Mark, Black Velvet, Southern Comfort… Hey, Joe. I'm not a drunk. I'll be fine. You know I can handle whatever life throws at me."

"Yes, I know that. And I also know you are going to 'retire' to your new old home in Montana, at least temporarily. You'll be living on your own, though, since the caretaker decided to move to Costa Rica. So..."

"Damn! I knew I was paying him too much."

Joe put up his hand. "Yes, maybe, but that's not what I'm telling you. Neither the doctor nor I want you to be alone while you're recovering."

"You're not sending some big-butted nurse to boss me around in my own home, torturing me with physical therapy…"

Joe grabbed William's flailing good arm to slow his excitement. "No, you'll have to be *chauffeured* into town to visit your big-butted nurse for physical therapy torture. I've arranged for a mechanic to stay there to keep an eye on you and help with repairs. Abe's the best around."

"Hmm. Well, set me up with a freezer full of frozen meals, a well-stocked liquor cabinet, and the last three years of Car and Driver magazine. I'll be good until one of those three runs out."

"Nope. You have a tractor or two that need bringing up to the twenty-first century, miles of fence line that needs to be maintained, and then those thrice-weekly trips to your PT torture."

"I hope you're going to tell me that's what Abe's for, because I don't do tractors, and I sure as hell don't run barbed wire…with or without a messed-up shoulder and three cracked ribs."

"Yes, that's what I'm telling you. And no. You will have your hands full with the physical therapy. No one can do that for you. Don't try to bail on those appointments, either. If you do, you'll lose the use of your left arm. I wouldn't look for Devine intervention on that one. I think you used up your lifetime supply of miracles in one big event. It's time for a little active participation on your part. Sort of a way for you to say thanks."

William looked toward the end of the bed, wiggled his toes, then looked to the sky. "Yes, thank You."

Chapter 2

Three days later
Backwaters of Alabama

Item: According to eyewitnesses of the spectacular fiery crash at Mesa Verde Speedway – aka Mesa Verde Park and Swap – last Saturday night, TV reality star William Gagnant was carried away from the wreckage by a supernatural entity. Initial reports said William's injuries were too severe to walk away from under his own power. Neither the show's producer, Joseph Patterson, nor Banner Hospital would report on the extent of his injuries, citing patient privacy.

***

"You're sure the job pays that much?" Abe asked, standing on the doorsteps of her trailer, as far as her corded phone would allow. "I mean, that sounds like a monthly salary, not weekly."

"Well, if you don't want it," Joe said, a wide smirk on his face, "I'll just hang up and call someone else."

"Oh, no you won't!" Dorothy called out as she burst into the room.

Joe turned around and faced the intruder. "Damn it, woman! Why do you think I have a separate office? You're not supposed to come in here when the door's closed."

"I'm your wife and this is my house, too. And it may be your business, but Abe is my aunt. She's perfect for this and you know it!"

"Hey, Dorothy," Abe said, her voice loud and clear through Joe's speaker phone, "I'll trust whatever you say. Do you think I should take the job? It sounds too good to be true."

"Yes, take it. Not only will it save you from having to buy another vehicle, but you can finally move out of that tin can travel trailer parked in that swamp you call home."

"But I like my privacy. You know that."

"Yes, I do." Dorothy shooed her husband out of his big office chair and took his place. "And I've been to this new place where I hope you'll be working soon. It's beyond being in the middle of nowhere. It's like being in the sticks beyond the sticks. There are wild horses – mustangs – there, too. Plus, not just the house, but everything there is huge! The shop is a mechanic's dream with tools practically dripping from the rafters."

"If it's so great, I'm surprised Joe didn't buy the place for himself," Abe said with a chuckle.

"Actually, he did. When I found out how far away it was from a major airport, I made him sell it. You know I don't do small planes, and I still have a few more countries to tick off on my must-see-before-I-die list."

"It's called a bucket list, Dorothy. So, what kind of work do I have to do for that much pay? It isn't illegal or immoral, is it?"

"No, no, no," Joe interjected. "Not fattening, either. There are a few pieces of equipment that need to be brought up to good-working order, and a possible project car if you're interested."

"Project car? What year, make, and model?" Abe gasped, unable to hide her excitement.

"That's a surprise. I guarantee you'll love it, though. Classic American, not one of those metric European cars with more electronics and plastic than metal."

"I'm on it! Where's the car? Can I drive there and pick it up? Is it in an English-speaking country? When can I leave?"

"Ah! I thought that might intrigue you. It's a project, remember? I'll have it shipped to you at your new job. How about you wrap up your affairs there in Alabama and pack? I'll have someone out there in a couple of days to pick up you and your motorcycle."

"Make it tomorrow morning at eight a.m. sharp. I don't have much to clean up, but I do want to give my Norton a tune-up and polish before shipping him to wherever we're going. By the way, where is it, anyhow?"

"A little place I like to call Forever, Montana. From the back porch of that estate, you can see forever."

"Sounds perfect."

"All right. Tomorrow morning at eight sharp I'll have you and the bike picked up. Oh, and don't worry about tools. The old foreman said that shop had every tool and goop ever created. If you can't cut it, torque it, glue it or weld it with what's there, you don't know what you're doing."

"Sounds like a challenge to me," Abe said brightly. Her tone lowered and she said sincerely, "Oh, and thanks. I was ready for a change."

Before Joe could reply, Dorothy jumped up and put her hand over his mouth. "We love you, darling," she called out to the speakerphone. "Tomorrow is the start of your grandest adventure."

"Yeah, right, Dorothy. You make me sound like Christopher Robin. Or would that be Pooh? Anyway, thanks again. Both of you."

Joe quickly pushed the end button on the desk phone and turned to his wife. "What was that all about?"

"You were going to say something about that idiot, weren't you?"

"Who? The one who dumped her after cleaning out her savings? Of course not. Well, except to say good riddance to bad rubbish…"

"See! That's why I butted in. Don't ever mention his name – or refer to him – again. That poor girl…"

"Girl, hell! She's your aunt!"

"Yes, but the same age as I am. She's barely forty-two and just getting ready for the second phase of her life. Who knows? Maybe she'll find her dream cowboy out there." Dorothy shook her head and frowned. "Maybe we shouldn't have found her a place so remote."

"Don't worry about her. She's smart enough to find her own happiness. Besides, I don't think she needs a man. Fixing up anything mechanical trips her trigger. No John Wayne or Roy Rogers required."

"Yeah, well, maybe not *required*, but sometimes a man in a ten-gallon hat is just what's *desired* to put a smile on a girl's face, no matter how old the girl. Come on, Joe. Let's go dig out that old Stetson. You can chase me around the bedroom until I let you catch me."

"Sounds like a mighty fine plan, ma'am," Joe drawled.

"That's Missy to you, pardner."

***

"Nope. Nope. Nuh-uh." Abe tossed items from the closet into a black plastic trash bag, rejecting clothes she'd worn for decades, previously too emotionally attached to them to throw them away. Well, today was the day to leave the past behind.

"Shoot, all I need are a few changes of undies, a couple of flannels, jeans, and a jacket. Oh, and let's not forget personal hygiene and appearance." She reached into the bathroom cabinet and swiped her toothbrush, toothpaste, deodorant, and hairbrush into a gallon-size baggie.

"Mama always did tell me to travel light. She just didn't know how low maintenance a woman could be." Abe tossed the bag of toiletries into the open backpack. "Now, is there anything in this old piece of trailer trash I can't live without?"

She dug through the small chest of drawers, pushing unmatched socks and torn tee-shirts out of the way. Her hand bumped into something solid: her battery-operated 'boyfriend.' She thought twice about whether to leave or bring the high-dollar dildo, then wrapped it up in a tank top and shoved the bundle into the backpack between the rolled-up socks and underwear.

"Whether I want you or not, my little smile-generator, I don't want Horace to find you when I give him this place for salvage." She shuddered at the thought of the grimy and grizzled old man in triple-patched coveralls. Once a month – twice during the holidays – he dropped by to see if she had scrap metal he could haul off. 'Or maybe there's something I can give – or share with – you,' he'd suggest if it was late in the day and he'd polished off his fifth of rheumatism medicine.

"I'd swear off sex entirely if he was the last man on earth." She patted the side of her backpack. "With or without batteries, you're still my favorite boyfriend, Titan."

The next morning, Abe was up at first light. It wasn't dawn's first pink glimmer through her lacy curtains that had disturbed her, though, but the nosing of a polecat digging in her trash.

Clank! Clatter!

"Damned skunk. I won't miss you," she grumbled soft enough to be heard but not enough to startle her daily visitor. "Well, maybe just a little bit," she admitted.

As if on cue, the little rascal turned to her voice and stood up on hind legs. One front paw swiped the air as if catching a wayward morsel.

"Yeah, goodbye to you, too, Pepé. I'm sure you'll find someone else who'll leave you scraps of food. Or you can go back to foraging for yourself. Thanks for not spraying. You have my permission to let loose with all you got when that junkman comes, though. Then again, your scent might be an improvement over his."

Pepé brought up his other paw and gave her a double-fisted goodbye. "Yeah, scoot. I have company coming soon. I don't want you to get run over, even if you are a varmint, kid."

Five minutes early, the truck pulled up. Rather than come into the most organized junkyard in the southern United States, the driver shut off the engine, took a drink from his oversized thermal mug of coffee, then disappeared beneath the dashboard.

"You don't have to wait until the clock strikes eight," Abe called out and waved him in.

The young driver popped back up, his eyes bright at seeing a new face. A woman in these backwoods was a treat to eyes and nose. Well, at least a woman without whiskers and a lower lip stained with chewing tobacco who didn't buy her clothes at Omar the Tentmakers.

"Who are you? I thought this place closed down years ago," the thirty-something father of three asked with a flirtatious grin.

"What difference does it make? I'm moving! And for good!" She stuck her key in the red, white, and blue Norton's ignition with a flourish, then kick-started it, pleased with its quick firing and hearty growl of perfect tuning.

"Pretty cool colors for a Harley," the man said with a wide grin, hoping to flatter her.

She huffed and shook her head, face down so he didn't see her scowl. Didn't he know this was a British motorcycle? Part of her wanted to correct him about the bike. Another part wanted to scold him for flirting – she'd noticed his wedding ring right away – but she bit back both comments. She needed his help to load her hefty vintage ride into the back of his flatbed.

"Got a way to get it up there?" she asked coolly.

"Oh, yeah…" He pulled a pair of ramps out from under the truck and set them at the tail end. He looked from them to her, then chuckled. "I guess I only need one, huh?"

"Yup. Just make sure the base is secure."

He took down the extra ramp and centered the other. He nudged it with the palm of his hand and said, "It's good."

Lips pursed, she shook her head and got off the bike. A quick jump onto the bottom of the ramp caused it to shift sideways.

"You have to dig it in first," she said. With gloved hands, she grabbed the expanded aluminum ramp, smacked it into the dusty red dirt, then tipped it forward onto the flat metal bed. She ran halfway up the ramp and back down. "Like that."

"Learn something new every day," he said and nodded politely. "Anything else I need to know, ma'am?"

She chuckled at his shift from flirting to being respectful. "Nah, I think you got it. Just make sure the parking brake is on."

"Oh, shit! Yeah…" He hopped in the truck, stomped the pedal, and called back. "Got it."

Abe gunned the engine and shot up the ramp, parking the '76 Norton Commando 850 smack dab in the middle of the flatbed. Kickstand set, she jumped down and began slinging tie downs to the driver, running to his side to position them and ratchet them tight. It was his truck but her prize riding atop it. She'd make sure it was secure.

"You know, I never thought a woman could do such a great job of tying down. Then again, I'm used to loading pallets and boxes, not motorcycles."

"Well, I'm sure if this was your ride, you'd be just as careful. Let me get my bag and I'll be ready. You're my chauffeur, too, right?"

"Well, I'm your ride to the airport. Nothing fancy about the front of my truck, although I did spend a minute after I pulled in, scraping all the trash into a bag."

"I'll bring a clean towel to lay down just in case there's some sticky stuff left. I can't be arriving at my new job all tacky. At least on the outside. What I am on the inside isn't going to change with moving 'cross country."

"Let's hope not," the driver said with a wide smile. "You are who you are, regardless of zip code."

"Amen and Hallelujah to that."

***

"Here you go, Abe," Joe said, giving her the front door key. "All the rest of them are in the key box, and I showed you where that was. Cyrus, the former caretaker, was fairly well organized. He put all the info on what's what and where – maintenance schedules, phone numbers, whatever – in this little pamphlet." He waved the folded and stapled three sheets of notebook paper in the air. "And I guess after you read this, you'll know more about this place than William."

"I don't know what you mean."

"You see, William is a traveling businessman of sorts. This may be his home, but he's never lived here. He did pop in to inspect the place before he bought it, but I don't think he's even spent one night here."

"Does he know about those mustangs you were talking about? Because what I know about horses – wild or otherwise – could fill an oat bucket."

"There's always the internet, Abe. Or you can call your niece."

"Joe, I don't do internet, only digital music. And when you call her

15

my niece, it makes me feel old. Please, just call her Dorothy or your wife. She's the same age as I am."

"Okay, Agatha…"

"Grr."

Joe laughed at her reaction to her legal first name. "By the way, I never told William you were a woman. He's always crowing about how he's such a liberal thinker, how he's a progressive and all. He only knows that Abe will be the mechanic here who will also drive him around if needed."

"I have to what?" she screeched.

"Drive him…"

"Yeah, yeah, yeah," she said, waving her hand in the air. "I said I'd come out, repair old tractors or whatnot. I'll even shovel horse crap if you want me to, but now you're saying I have to be cooped up in a car for a trip to the city once a week?"

"No," Joe said, trying to keep a straight face.

"No? What aren't you saying, Joe?"

"Is driving going to be a problem? I thought you could operate anything with two to eighteen wheels." He ducked as she threw a playful swing.

"I knew that was too much money for what you said."

"Sorry. I'll see if I can get you a raise if you'd like."

"Nah. I'm still making more than I was plus getting free room and board. Who would have thought that living in a modified barn could be so comfortable? Shoot, I'd have been happy to just be dry and cozy with inside plumbing. Money on top of that is just bonus bucks."

"Okay, you've got the general layout of the house and shop. Let's go upstairs and see your apartment."

At the top of the stairs, Joe opened the door and held his arm out dramatically for her to enter. "Your castle, m'lady."

"Wow…" Abe gushed as she walked in. "This is a shop apartment? With vaulted ceilings and a picture window?" She walked over and looked through the eight-foot-wide window at the windswept panorama. "And this doesn't even look out over the shop." She turned back to Joe. "A view like this is worth a couple hundred itself."

Joe chuckled. "You know, Cyrus said if he hadn't got such a great deal on a condo in Costa Rica, he wouldn't have left. Maybe I shouldn't tell you, but I will since you're already here. Montana winters are brutal but with three kinds of heat available – propane, wood, and electric – and the right kind of clothing, you'll be fine. Summers can be hot, but Cyrus said getting chores done early in the day takes care of most of that problem. After that, just kick back, watch TV, and let the air conditioner do its magic."

"Or read a book," Abe said.

"Oh, that's right." Joe grinned wide, remembering the reason he had wanted Abe for the job. She knew nothing of pop culture and its stars. "There's a library in town. If they can't find a book you're looking for, let me know and I'll get you fixed up."

Joe walked through the kitchen, turning the faucet on, then shutting it off. "Household repairs are taken care of by a local outfit. For everything else, there's a list of contractors and who does what in that little binder under the fax machine on the desk. A housekeeper comes in once a week to clean up and do laundry and stock the pantry as needed.

"As for the horses, there are only a few daring mustangs that come all the way in to feed. They were born in the wild and are used to the harsh climate. They don't need sheltering. When I was here, I bribed them with sweetened oats in the evening just so they'd come in from pasture. It's a good idea to make sure they aren't too afraid of humans. You don't want them too skittish for their annual vet checkups, vaccines, and such."

"Like I said, Joe, I don't know anything about horses."

"You don't need to unless you want to ride them. All they do around here is eat, shit, and breed. These guys and gals are not much more than scenery: mobile bits of the landscape."

"I thought they were rescues."

"They were and are. They don't need anything. I only bring out the oats so I can watch them come in, majestic and proud, not to try and tame them. Don't worry about them. They'll be fine. All you're expected to do is get William to and from his appointments. Taking care of the stuff around here with gears, wheels, and motors is more of a distraction for you. Feeding the mustangs treats isn't a chore. I consider it a pleasant diversion."

Joe dabbed under his eyes, trying to wipe away the sadness of losing the huge pets that had been his for less than a month. "By the way, there's a side-by-side four-wheeler in the shop that's been giving Cyrus fits. He said he wanted to convert it from a gas motor to an electric one. Something about wanting a quiet way to sneak up on wildlife to get a better view or something."

"Power conversion? Oh, how I love a challenge!" Abe sang out. She twirled in place and touched one big toe to the opposite knee – a perfect pirouette in denim and plaid – then plopped back spread-eagle onto the king-sized bed.

"This has got to be the biggest one-bedroom apartment ever built." She leaned over onto one elbow and looked out the smaller but still big bedroom window. "Awesome! And maid service to boot!"

"Well, if you have it under control," Joe said, "I think I'm going to hit the road. Oh, here's that cell phone. You left it in the car. I know you didn't have one in the bayou, but it's not just you here. Or not all the time. William will be back to world traveling once he gets healed, only here a few weeks a year. The rest of the time, you'll be flying solo, the lady in charge of this big place. And keep this phone with you. If you get hurt, you need to be able to call for help."

Abe rolled her eyes and grinned. "Big place? Hell, it's huge. Got it. And I'll keep the phone with me. Do you want me to walk out with you?"

Joe scoffed. "No. I think I'll walk around ands check it out one more time by myself. If I didn't love my wife so much, I wouldn't have given it up."

"But you didn't really – give it up."

"I sold it at cost if that's what you mean."

"No, you sold it to your business partner so you could pop in every once in a while." Abe shrugged. "I'd say that was a pretty smart move." She put one hand on his shoulder, looking away from the tears she saw welling in his eyes. "Hey, you take it easy. Don't work long hours. I'm sure I'll see you around again soon."

Joe nodded in agreement, too emotional to speak. He looked out the window, taking it in one last time. A huge panorama of cumulous clouds was billowing up in an energetic display of grays and whites. "You can count on it."

He headed to the door, sniffing. "I gotta go before I get weepy. I'll call later."

"See ya!" she chirped, hoping her upbeat tone would make him feel better. "Saying goodbye sounds too final."

"See ya," he answered back, and then was gone.

Yes, he'd left William in good hands.

***

Abe bounced into the kitchen to see what treasures were there. Not that she liked to cook, but she did like to eat. She opened the refrigerator and saw the staples: bread, milk, juice, and bagged salad. In the freezer were packs of frozen fruits and veggies, a few various types of meats, and several pints of assorted ice creams. On the breakfast bar was a fruit bowl with a piece of paper wedged between an apple and a banana.

Abe read the note aloud. "'Just fax me a grocery list by Tuesday and I'll bring what you want with me on Thursday morning. Welcome to Forever, Montana! The Home Team. Fax 406-555-1212.'

"I think I died and went to heaven," Abe squealed. She looked over and saw it again. This time, she reached out and tried to touch both sides of the picture window. "Well over five-and-a-half feet wide. Mama always did say good things come to those who wait. Just because I had to wait forty years doesn't mean this place is any less appreciated. Shoot, I love it even more!"

Grabbing her backpack, Abe stepped into the bedroom and dropped it by the bed, claiming the new domain for herself. Holding her breath, she tiptoed to the closet, pulled the door open quickly, then laughed at herself. "Yeah, right. As if someone would stash a Class A manfriend for me out here in the sticks. Or that he'd disappear if I opened the door too slowly."

Bzzz. Bzzz.

"What the heck?" Abe followed the noise to the front door. Sitting on the long, narrow entry room table was her cell phone, vibrating away. She picked it up. "Hello?"

"Is that you, Agatha?" Joe asked.

"Grrr!"

Joe laughed out loud then brought himself back to the conversation. "Sorry 'bout that, Abe. I got distracted earlier. I forgot to make sure you had your driver's license. I think you might need it."

"Of course."

"Of course? Which one, of course?" Joe asked.

"Both. Of course, I have it. It's the ID I used for the plane ride here. And of course, I'll need it. You're having my Snortin' Norton shipped here still, right? If you tell me no, you're going to ruin my perfect day."

"Yes and maybe no."

"Yes and no? Which one yes and which one no?"

"Yes, I'm shipping your bike there. And yes or maybe no, I don't know if I'm going to ruin your day. And before we go back and forth on yesses and noses, fingers and toes-es, let me tell you more about that one little clause on the contract you signed."

"Contract?"

"Yes, contract. You know, the one I had you sign before you flew out this morning."

"I didn't sign any contract!" Abe bristled. "I just signed for the tickets I picked up at the airlines."

"A signature almost always means a contract of one sort or another. That's Business 101. You agreed to assist in care and maintenance of the Forever View Ranch in exchange for salary, room and board, and any other amenities as may be offered. Thirty day minimum fulfillment. Terms and conditions may apply."

"What's that mean?" Abe asked, eyes narrow as she reached for the biggest piece of fruit in the dish, ready to smash it through the receiver.

"Pretty much that you have to do what I need for no less than one month. That's one of the longer months, not February in case you were curious."

Abe tapped the speaker icon and tossed the phone down, too irritated to hold onto it. She grunted, walked toward the door, then changed her mind and came back. Twice. Three times.

Joe heard the clunk and then the pacing. "I hate to pull a fast one on you, Abe, but I'm in a predicament. That place can pretty much run itself with a manager to coordinate outsourced labor. What I really need is for you to take the kindly old gentleman who owns this place to a few physical therapy appointments after he gets here. Nothing else."

"No cooking or cleaning?"

"Nope," he said.

"No diaper changes, spoon-feeding, or sponge baths?"

"Nope. William is my business associate and a great guy. He isn't infirm or incontinent, either. He was in a horrible car crash, Abe. He broke a few ribs, dislocated his leg, and required some shoulder surgery. He also got all the bumps, bruises, aches, and pains that go with being in a wreck. I don't trust him to drive himself to his appointments. Since the housekeeper only shows up once a week and well..." Joe cleared his throat and continued, hoping Abe hadn't noticed how flustered he had become. "Anyhow, she's only there once a week and very busy."

"And said housekeeper can't stand the old coot, but the money for cleaning up and stocking the larder is too good to turn away."

Joe chuckled. "What can I say? It's an employees' market these days. Why drive half a day to get to the edge of the earth if it isn't for twice the usual pay? Still, whether he could manage himself or not, I'd feel better if someone accompanied him."

"Which means said old coot doesn't want to go to physical therapy sessions because they hurt. And he's stubborn. Or both. Hey, wait. You're not going to tell me he's some crazy drug addict, too, are you? Do I need to carry a gun because if so, I'm in trouble. I sold the only one I had because I couldn't bring it on the airplane with me."

"William is harmless. He and I have worked together for years. He's one of those British business partner fellows I told you about."

"Joe, you never told me anything about your business or partners, British or otherwise. All I know is Dorothy crows about how happy she is that you're an international businessman. When you go off into some God-forsaken place for a month, she can travel somewhere civilized without guilt. Both of you are happy apart and neither one of you seem to mind the separation. She said when you're in town, you two are together so much, you both look forward to your next trips abroad."

"Well, she does have that right. I guess what my career entails doesn't make a difference..."

Abe put up her hand as if he was there and could see it and interrupted. "Unless that business is illegal or immoral. I can deal with fattening, but not those other two. Nuh-uh."

"Totally legal," Joe assured her. "But as I said, I care a great deal for William. I guess he's as much a friend as a business associate."

"But an obnoxious turd."

"Now, why would you say that, Abe? I didn't ask you to come all the way out to the pucker-brush because you have the thickest skin of any person – male or female – I've ever met," he said, then added softly, "although that might help."

Abe ignored his dig and added her own. "But because I'm your wife's favorite aunt, right?"

"Actually, that's part of it. However, most of it is because you're the best mechanic I could find who might be willing to come out to the vast wilderness of Montana."

"And who wouldn't try to buy up the ground beneath her feet that you love so much once she got here."

"No. One who wouldn't run away at the first frozen windshield or even ten-foot-high snowdrift. Dang it, Agatha – I mean, Abe – this country is just like you. And that stockpile of goodies I have coming in... Well, I can't wait to see what you'll do with them."

"What goodies? Coming in when? You mean the project? No, no, never mind. I can't get anxious *or* disappointed if I don't know what I'm missing."

"Well, here's a hint. Can you say classic vintage sportscar?" Joe crooned through the line.

"American or foreign? Wait. Stop. You weren't messing with me yesterday about sending a car, were you? Or are you at it again? Stop teasing me with the juiciest carrots you can find. You know I like my bikes and cars old and fast. What I remember you saying was something about electrifying an old gas-powered four-wheeler to go off-road."

"But what I'm sending you would be more fun *on* road," he teased.

Abe looked around the room again, taking in the convenience and luxury of her new surroundings. What difference did it make if she had to put up with a black and blue British businessman? She didn't have anything to go back to even if she did want to return to her near-starvation existence at the swamp. She hadn't had much more than lawnmowers and chainsaw tuneups for the last month. Plus, she'd given away her trailer for scrap.

"Yeah, sure. I'll stick around and take this guy to the leg puller or arm twister or whatever you call 'em, Joe. I don't have much else to do here. I never learned to knit or crochet. TV and old movies aren't my style, and I never learned to garden. Whatever projects come my way will be appreciated. I'm not one to bite the hand that feeds me. Or that of his British tea bag buddy."

"That's my girl. I'm bringing William out there myself in a few days. I'll need some help unloading his luggage and wheelchair when I get there. After that, you're free to go. I mean, to stay and do whatever it is you want to do. But I want you to be on hand. In case he falls, or..." Joe took a deep breath and began again. "Sorry about the babbling. I need to get some sleep. It's been a rough few days, and I still have a long day of connections and flights ahead of me."

"At your service, boss."

"I'm not the boss. Rather, I'm not the one you have to keep happy. That would be William."

"Happy? How about if we settle on not pissing him off so much that he tosses me out in the next thirty days of our contract?"

"What?"

Abe waved the note about the grocery list in the air. "This contract I signed. You do know contracts go both ways, right? According to this, you can't get rid of me without thirty days written notice. No shortcuts, Joe. I sacrificed a lot coming out at the last minute. Security is the least you can give me."

Joe shuffled papers on the front seat of his car, looking for a copy of the quickie contract he had downloaded from the internet. "Damn. I mean, Darned tootin'. I have you covered for the next month, at least. William *needs* someone there for a few weeks to transport him to appointments, but if he finds out how great your mechanical skills are, he'll want you around for more than a month."

"Well then," Abe said, setting the pretend contract down next to the fax machine, "I guess I'll just have to make myself and my works so invaluable, he'll have no choice but to hire me full time."

"See, I always knew you were a smart woman."

"Person. Smarts aren't gender dependent."

"As you are fond of saying, Amen and Hallelujah to that."

Chapter 3

One week later

News Item: Another mystery in the 'Angel or Alien?' drama is unfolding after the disappearance of the miracle survivor of the fiery car crash, William Gagnant. The reality TV star was released from the hospital in the wee hours this morning and no word on where he went. An enterprising entrepreneur has set up a crowdfunding account to sponsor a reward for finding him and getting an interview. Fans are encouraged to donate to the 'Find Our Guy' Fund. Monies from the FOG Fund will be given to whoever finds William…less administration fees, of course.

***

Queens, New York
Psychiatric Evaluation Center

'Duz anyone know where our guy is?' Eddie 'Razor' Rizzo posted again on the 'Around the World in 80 Cars' fan page.

Finally, a reply that wasn't a 'stop spamming the site' or an attempt to block him came through.

'If they do, they're not saying,' Ford Fan typed in. After a moment, he added, 'But I have an idea where he went. Got no wheels, tho.'

'PM me,' Razor answered. He waited on the floor in the coat closet, knees up, biting his nails until the screen lit up with a reply.

'Ford Fan here. What's up?'

'What yur idea?' Razor typed in.

'Where are you?' Ford replied. 'If you're close, we can go together.'

'In NYC area. Close enough?'

'Meet me at Chuckie's Cheesecake Donuts in Queens. Wear a Ford ballcap and red shirt so I'll know you.'

'When?' Ford typed back.

'When can U B there?'

'One hour.'

'Make it 2. Look for a dark blue '98 Focus with custom wheels.'

'Done deal.'

Razor snapped the vintage cell phone closed. No one at the clinic knew he had a phone and they never would. He patted the keys he had lifted an hour earlier. He was going to walk away from this nuthouse today no matter what. Legally, they couldn't keep him longer since he'd been cooperative. He knew his rights. Besides, he wasn't stealing the Focus, he was just borrowing it from the doc for a test drive. He'd return it – or at least leave it where it could be found – when he was done with it.

Sniffing with disgust, he looked around the recreation room of the psychiatric hospital one last time. It hadn't been as bad as he thought it'd be. Tables of puzzles, board games, and a library of VHS tapes and old TVs filled the room. Not one item that related to the real world or current events was here, though. The docs and nurses said that might upset some of their 'clients.'

The other residents there were mostly mellow and eager to please him, the new guy. Telling them that he was William Gagnant's brother got him a lot of respect. He left off that he was his spiritual, not biological, brother. They wouldn't have understood anyhow. Especially since they were idiots and didn't know who William Gagnant was. He didn't disagree when one old man thought Gagnant was the president of England. He gave him his desserts in exchange for stories about when he and William were kids, playing gigs in Liverpool with the Beatles. Nobody cared enough about anyone else to disagree, so they all got along. Mostly oblivious, but safe enough.

His best day ever was when he convinced that schizophrenic computer hacker to bypass the security block on the ancient computer used for playing solitaire. It didn't take much and the video was uploaded, the one he'd shot of his spiritual brother's rescue by aliens.

Or was it by angels? He wasn't sure. Maybe it was an alien angel.

Either way, it was a good thing the hacker guy could access the file from The Cloud. Not having his smartphone was the pits. Raising a stink about it would have kept him there for another month, though. He'd play nice until he got his break, checking posts on message boards with the old analog cell phone.

He'd lost track of time but knew it had been more than a week since William had crashed. He had to find him. If this 'Ford Fan' could help him, he'd split the reward money everyone on the message board was talking about. Then he and his spiritual brother could travel the world racing and fixing up cars together. Finally.

***

Two hours later

A young man with a red Ford ballcap stepped out of the doorway to the blue Focus. "Are you Razor?"

"I am if you're Ford Fan," Razor said, leaning across the passenger seat to open the door.

Ford touched the brim of his hat and nodded. "First things first. If I tell you what I know, we'll split the pot fifty-fifty."

"As long as we're splitting the cost of the road trip fifty-fifty. This ride don't run on just my good looks."

Ford pulled the door open and climbed in. "Deal. Get on the highway and head west. My sources say he's on his way to Montana."

"Where in Montana?" Razor asked.

"I'd be an idiot if I told you now," Ford said. "Just drive. I'll pay for the next fill up, you get the one after that." Ford looked at the pot belly on the twenty-ish man behind the wheel and added, "And we buy our own food."

***

Meanwhile, in Montana

"Do you know when you'll get here?" Abe asked.

"Hold on," Joe said, then took his phone off speaker mode. He looked in the back seat to see if one-third of his hit TV show

27

phenomenon was still loopy. Yes, William's eyes were shut, fluttering as he dreamed. He hadn't heard the feminine voice come through.

"We're on our way there now. The hospital wanted to keep him another day, but William was insistent that he knew his body better than they did. I'd say we have an ETA of about twenty minutes. Make sure his bed is made and there are plenty of pillows. Oh, and it would be nice if you had a pot of soup simmering or a pie baking. You know, to make the house smell good."

"What?" she screeched. "I'm not the housekeeper! And my cooking talents don't go beyond microwaving popcorn!"

Joe pulled the phone away from his ear, glad he had taken her off speakerphone. Her rant would have awakened William, for sure. "Now, now, dear…"

"Don't call me dear!" she hissed. A heron flew past her apartment window and a wave of peace settled over her. "I know, I know. I'm getting compensated very well for this, but I didn't hire on…"

"Canned soup is fine," Joe interjected. "I'm sure there's plenty in the pantry. The bed should already be made, but make sure the house is warm. He's not moving about much. I don't want him to catch a chill on top of everything else. Sneezing could be disastrous with his broken ribs."

"I'm on it. I'll be here to help you bring him into the house and get settled. Just honk the horn in case I don't hear you pull up because I'm fluffing pillows and vacuuming."

"Ha, ha," Joe said dryly. "Over and out."

"Who was that?" William asked.

"Who? Oh, I thought you were asleep."

"Not enough drugs in my system for that. Sounds like you have a housewarming party all set up."

Joe went over his brief conversation with Abe in his head, wondering if he had mentioned anything that would have given away her gender. No. "Just the help. We're only about twenty minutes away…"

"So I heard," William said, then grunted as Joe hit a pothole.

"Oops. Sorry. The gent at the rental agency said this car had the best suspension. I guess I should have consulted Morris or Ben instead."

"Any Bentley would have beaten this over-rated and undersized Chevrolet. Where'd you get this heap of rubbish anyway? And what model is it?"

Joe inhaled, unable to answer. He had called the first car rental company that popped up in the search engine and asked for a comfortable ride. He hadn't even noticed the Chevrolet insignia embossed in the middle of the steering wheel until William complained. He had no idea what body style it was, so ignored the question. "I want you to stop thinking about cars. Start concentrating on getting stronger and back into shape."

William started to laugh but was brought up short by rib pain. He groaned and coughed softly. "I've never been strong or in shape, so there's no going 'back' to it. And I'm too bloody old for a body make-over. I think you have the right idea with this," William waved his hand at the verdant grasslands outside the window, "sending me out to pasture with the horses."

"Hey, hey, hey. Everyone in your family has lived into their nineties. By that reckoning, you're just approaching middle age. You were certainly acting like it, racing your mid-life crisis dream car around that damned old track. I thought that place had been decommissioned."

"It was. Its glory days ended twenty years ago. It's been used as a park and swap site for the past decade, at least. I talked the owners into letting us have it while it was 'closed for repairs.'"

"What?" Joe screeched, slamming on the brakes, sending William forward.

"Dammit, Joe! Are you trying to kill me, or just hurt me so bad that I want to kill you?"

"I knew that track looked like shit. You're not kidding, are you? It really hasn't been active on the racing circuit for twenty years?"

"Closer to thirty. That oval was the main attraction around there for decades – big fish in a small pond and all that nonsense. When its popularity dried up to a puny puddle, the owners found another use for it. I didn't think you'd check it out too closely since it was so far west and in the pucker-brush. I guess I was right."

"That was not my job," Joe hissed, biting off a five-minute tirade that wouldn't make a dent in his star's stainless-steel armor of self-righteousness.

William chuckled, softly enough that it didn't hurt but loud enough for his show's producer to hear. He knew he was right, so no use wasting precious breath.

"Well, it's the task of one of my associate producers, but not me directly," Joe admitted.

"What do they say out here in America? The buck stops here?" William pointed out the window. "Or maybe the bull stops here. More cattle than wildlife by the looks of it."

"We'll see what it's like in a few miles once we're past irrigated fields. Your place is out in what you call 'the pucker-brush.' There are more elk, deer, and antelope than cows in your neighborhood."

"And no paparazzi. You did say no one knows where I'm recuperating, right?"

"I only told Morris and Ben, but don't worry about them. They're busy, working on a special project."

"What?" William asked sarcastically. "Driving trucks loaded with cases of whiskey through an obstacle course on a volcanic field in Iceland? The fastest time without losing his liquid cargo gets to keep what's left?"

"Hey, that's a great idea, but no. I told them to develop seven themes for next season. Actually, I told them twenty. When they're done, I'll pare those down to seven. I already have a few ideas of my own. This way, they keep busy, feel like they're contributing to the program, plus they're keeping out of trouble."

"And earning their salary," William huffed.

"Don't worry. You're getting paid while on recovery and you don't even have to think about the show or cars."

"Paid? I don't care about money. I just want to be able to take a whiz by myself and do it without excruciating pain."

"It hurts when you urinate?"

"No, but when I get out of bed to use a proper toilet, it does. Remind me not to do something this stupid again."

"You? I don't think anyone could even begin to convince you to keep away from vehicles or motors or racetracks or…"

William raised one hand and winced. "Maybe the first two, but I've lost my love for racetracks."

"Yeah, right," Joe said. "I don't believe that for a moment. That's the drugs speaking."

"No, actually, it's not. I haven't had any all day. But I do want to clarify."

"Yes…"

"I am absolutely done, over, fed up with – and any other way you want to parse it – ancient, crumbling racetracks, no matter what mode of transportation you propose to use."

"So, no chariot racing in Rome at the Coliseum. Got it." Joe took one hand off the steering wheel and checked off an imaginary list.

William looked out at the vast expanse of nothingness. No, not nothingness. The plains were dotted with golden vegetation, some clustered together like little islands in the ocean, others lined up alongside dried-up remnants of what had, at one time, been a seasonal water source. "Is there a drought?" he asked.

"I think the whole world has either been in drought or flood for the last five years. Unfortunately for the animals and vegetation, this is the drier half of the earth."

"As long as there's enough water to make ice and electricity, I'll be fine."

Joe hit a dip in the road, jostling the car. "Oops. Sorry."

"Ice and whiskey," William amended.

"Last I heard, you don't need water to make whiskey. It's distilled from various grains…"

"Oh, please don't talk," William groaned.

"You're right. But corn, rye, barley…all grains need water to grow." Joe paused at the lack of response. "Okay. Enough about that. Just for the record, we only have about twenty minutes to go, then you'll get to meet your new mechanic and chauffeur, Abe."

"Here's hoping he's not as chatty as you are. I'm ready for the peace and quiet you promised when you talked me into buying this place."

"Uh-huh," Joe said, nodding. *Yup. Now is absolutely the time to stop talking. No need to make a correction to the 'he's not as chatty' remark. He'll find out soon enough that Abe is a she.*

***

Joe slowed to a stop as gently as possible. However, there was no way to smooth out the cobblestone drive to the house other than to drive over the well-manicured lawn.

"Are you trying to hit every bump, Joe? I think you may have missed a few. Do you want to turn around and try again?"

Joe looked at his watch, then back at the gray-faced William. "I think you're overdue for your pain meds. You're crankier than a baby without a bottle."

"I'm not a baby but right now, I'm ready for a bottle. A big one and an ice-filled tumbler with a bucket of same next to it. The doc said I can't take pain pills and drink at the same time, so I decided I'll stick with the latter. It's easier to get refills on booze when it runs out."

"As long as you can get through your physical therapy regimen and be back on the show in six weeks, I'll make sure you have all the liquor you need. Or rather, want."

Joe noticed the curtain move in the huge picture window in the front of the house. A second later, half of the double front door opened. Abe was ready for performing curbside assistance. He inhaled deeply, held his breath, then let it all out in a slow and steady – and hopefully calming – breath.

"What's wrong with you, Joe? Asthma?"

Startled by William adding genuine concern to his recent blend of

32

rage and sarcasm, Joe answered, "No, actually, I'm just bracing myself. This is going to take a lot of effort on your part. I can hire all the nurses and aides in this valley, stock you with whatever booze or pain pills you think will get you through this, but in the end, it's all up to you. Please, whether you decide to come back to the show or not, take care of yourself. You need to heal completely. No shortcuts on therapy or ignoring it entirely. This new journey you're on is tougher than a week in the Gobi with those two wingnuts harassing you, driving a bare-bones kit car, and living on boil-in-the-bag rations."

"Wingnuts?" William asked sourly. "You're not sending Little Ben and Morris the Monster to assist in my recovery, are you?" He sniffed back an unexpected tear at Joe's sincerity.

Joe shook his head but didn't reply. He got out of the car, then leaned in and told William, "This journey's a solo adventure, mate. You have a bit of technical assistance, but it's only your heart and spirit that will get you through this healing process."

William chuckled, uncomfortable at the affection flooding the interior of the Chevy sedan. "You mean my spirit and spirits. Where is that bottle?" he asked with a forced smile.

As Joe shut the door, he saw Abe was at the back of the car, waiting for instructions on which to handle first: the passenger or the luggage. Joe nodded to the trunk. "We'll need the wheelchair first, Abe."

Abe found a souvenir ball cap in the trunk and bit off the tag. She bent over and shoved her hair under the cap. A quick tug on the brim and her disguise was in place. Pushing aside the two pieces of luggage, she grabbed the folded-up wheelchair and set it on the ground. She pulled it open and unsnapped her denim overshirt in one fluid motion, clouding her female form in a billow of blue. She chuffed in self-admonishment at her lame deception. Her new boss would find out soon enough he had a woman working for him. Still, if he was in pain from surgery and the long ride home, it would be best not to shock him right away.

Then again, if she did this right, he'd never find out. For his six weeks of recovery, she could handle tasks out of sight or at least in limited, ill-defined light. The ball-capped driver didn't have to speak much, if at all. Get him healed, out the door, and back to work in whatever international business he and Joe were involved with.

Then she could get on with this new chapter in her life.

She already knew she wanted to stay here forever. Not only was the pay fantastic, but her apartment was yummier than she could have dreamt up. It was the ambiance, though – the scent of sage and motor oil – that made her feel as if she belonged here. She could remain aloof and in the other building until William healed and left to go back to work again. It shouldn't be hard to keep any necessary conversations to short grunts or gestures with hands covered in work gloves.

She pushed the wheelchair toward Joe and tried on her new persona. "Here," she said, her voice forced low, then stepped back out of anyone's view. She was near if Joe needed assistance, but she didn't need to be on display as 'the female' help. The muscle on standby in the shadows was better.

Joe rolled the wheelchair close to the passenger door and set the brakes. His hands twitched, ready to offer support, to make sure William didn't slip or falter. He knew better than to get in the proud man's face while he tried to get out, though.

Involuntary grunts and stifled groans escaped as William – more frail than ever – grasped the door handle for support.

Abe watched as William struggled, both in his effort to exit the car and his determination not to lose his dignity. The silver-haired man kept his head down as he progressed, deep in concentration, his teeth clenched to prevent yelps of pain. She could have been standing directly in front of him – buck naked with bells hanging from her nipples and a football helmet on her head – and he wouldn't have seen her.

"Let me help…" Joe began, then quickly shut up as he realized he was insulting William with the offer of assistance.

The man's guttural growl followed by, "I got this," said a lot about him. William was one determined – and most likely very onery – man

34

who was used to doing everything his way. Abe noted the summation of the shortcut personality test. Don't even try to talk this man into – or out of – anything.

That might not be the only reason William was still a bachelor, but it was a major one.

***

"Do you have everything you need?" Joe asked, pushing William and his wheelchair into the elaborate game room area.

William turned his head and glared, one eye squinted in pain. "Medicine. Old World medicine in a glass with ice cubes."

"Oh, yes, that's right. Let's see what we have in here, shall we?"

Joe scanned every flat surface in the room, looking for the soup he'd asked Abe to fix. He picked up the brushed aluminum thermos on the bar, sniffed it, and verified it wasn't coffee. "It looks like Abe fixed some soup. Nice and hot."

"Probably out of a can," William groused. "Doesn't make a difference whether it is or isn't. You told me…"

Joe rushed over to the occasional table he had parked William next to and set the thermos down. "It's more of a broth, I believe," he assumed, swishing it to see if the contents were liquid or solid. "No spoon required."

He set it back down. "Honestly, William. I don't mind if you numb your pain with alcohol, but please don't put it in an empty stomach. You need sustenance, and malted barley isn't it. Promise me you'll eat at least two healthy meals a day. Abe is a decent cook."

"I can cook for myself," William grunted as he reached for the thermos, nearly knocking it to the floor before he got a good hold. After struggling for a moment, he figured out how to get the cap off. "Damned lids. They ought to label them screw-on or pop-off." He sniffed the contents, raised an appreciative eyebrow, then chugged it down.

"One meal down, one to go. And there were peas and rice in that broth, so that counts as a balanced meal, not a drink. Now, where's my

35

whisky?"

Joe looked around and saw Abe pointing to a stained-glass image of an owl. *Wise girl, she's still out of William's line of vision.* "Uh, I think it's here." Joe tugged on the side edge of the 'picture frame' and the decorative glass door swung open.

"Clear or brown?" he asked, holding a bottle of whisky in one hand, tequila in the other.

"Brown? Bourbon if you have it, straight whisky if not. And bring the whole bottle. Just because I can walk doesn't mean I want to traipse back and forth, refilling my glass every few minutes."

Joe dropped two ice cubes into a glass and brought it over with the whisky. After he poured out William's drink, he lifted the bottle in a toast. "Here's to a fast recovery. I'd join you, but I'm driving. I have to make a quick turnaround. My darling wife made reservations for us, and I have to make it back to the airport this evening. Something about our twentieth wedding anniversary."

"Twenty years? You've been with the same woman for that long?"

"When it's right, it doesn't seem that long, William. You'll see what I mean when you find your Mrs. Right."

"If I find her, I can guarantee one thing."

"What's that?"

"If she's a Mrs. Wright, I won't have anything to do with her. I don't date married women."

"I'll salute that," Joe said and clinked the bottle of bourbon to William's glass.

William slugged down the contents, then held out the glass for more. "It didn't even have a chance to get chilled. I guess I'll make the next one last longer."

"I sure hope so." Joe poured the drink, then set the bottle down and looked up at Abe. "All the luggage out of the car and into his room?"

She nodded in reply, swishing an impish smirk at keeping silent.

Joe looked at William. "Anything you need before I go? Ping pong paddles, ice skates, a hula hoop or two?"

William snorted in reply. "I have no energy for sports, even after my three-course dinner of chicken, wild rice, and sautéed vegetables. Just hand me the remote control and get out of here. Give that wife of yours a big hug for me. Lord knows I couldn't so much as shake hands with her if she were here."

"Will do. You do remember where your room is, right?"

"Give me a break. I'm bent and broken, not old and senile." William's eyes went side to side. Suddenly, he was disoriented. He hadn't been in this house more than two days since he bought it a year ago and hadn't even slept in it.

"It's down this hall," Joe said softly, winking. "And there aren't any stairs in the house, so no excuse for falling down. Besides, we don't have a medic standing by."

"Or cameras," William chuckled. "I guess that means I can run around naked if I want to."

Joe looked up and saw that – just as he expected – Abe's eyes were wide in shock. "Nope."

"Why not?"

"William, I don't think you'll be 'running around' anywhere for a few weeks, at least. Toddling, maybe, or using a cane, probably. But if I were you, I'd keep clothes on wherever you go. If you do happen to take a tumble and an ambulance comes to pick you up, it'll be a hell of a chore to get trousers on over a broken leg."

Joe saw Abe's sigh of relief out of the corner of his eye and heard William's mock gasp of shock at the same time. He patted the beleaguered man's back. "You'll be safe here, I'm sure. I've left you in good hands. But remember, the healing is up to you. And you alone. Your body is going to mend, but whether it mends straight or crooked, mobile or pinned to that wheelchair for the rest of your life will be the result of how much effort you put into your physical therapy."

"Thanks for the pep talk. Now get out of here. I don't have to go anywhere for two days, right?"

"The doctor only gave you one day to recuperate from traveling." Joe looked at the clock on his smartphone and grinned. "With all this settling in and arranging your 'medicine' cabinet, that's twenty-three and a half hours from now."

"Well, allowing for seven or eight hours of sleep – and at a rate of one bottle every three hours…" William looked at his watch and chuckled. "That means about five bottles to go."

"Don't count on it. I've hidden your stash of pain relief in various spots around here. After your appointment tomorrow, give me a call. Tell me how it went, and I'll let you know where the next bottle is."

Abe gasped at the plan. She knew nothing of it. She was sure to be caught in the middle. She knew how mean an angry drunk deprived of his booze was. She couldn't see William's face for his reaction, but she could see his body language. His initial tension had relaxed. He had an ace up his sleeve.

Or so he thought.

Joe watched as William's horror flipped to self-assurance. "And don't think you can call in for more booze. I got that covered."

"Don't worry about me. I'll be the model patient for this Montana doc. I'll be fit as a fiddle and two times as sweet at least three weeks before it's time to hit the road again. Mark my words."

"Marked," Joe said. He glanced at Abe and saw her shrug. She didn't have an idea of what he was talking about, either.

"Why don't you do me a favor and bring out my other bottle now, Joe. You have a plane to catch, and I'm sure Abe has places to go and things to do, too."

Before Joe could reply, Abe grunted and left through the kitchen, out of view of William.

"See ya, Abe," Joe called out after her. Out of habit, he started to tell her to take care but caught his breath instead.

Would one man say that to another? Nah. The less said, the better. Let William find out the truth later.

Much later.

Chapter 4

Find Our Guy Reward tops $300,000! It seems everyone has joined the latest rage: searching for William Gagnant. Bookies in Vegas are laying thirty to one odds that the star of Around the World in 80 Cars will be found in the next twenty-four hours. The highest odds are that he is secluded on one of the most inaccessible places in Great Britain, Swona Island, part of the Orkney Island chain north of Scotland. Stay tuned. Updates posted as they happen.

***

William set his head in his hand and rolled it side to side as if frustrated or in pain. He didn't want Joe to see he was hiding a laugh.

He would have to be blind not to see that 'Abe' was a woman. Well, not blind but oblivious to his surroundings. In all honesty, he probably had been, but not as much as Joe thought.

The first signal about her gender was all from Joe. He had been too quick to take the phone call off speakerphone. He'd also slipped and called her dear. He could practically hear the worry lines pop out as his producer carefully chose his words. And when asked to shut up, he had!

The second hint was the blatant lack of 'welcome back to your new home.' Joe was so proud of this place and bragged about how friendly and happy everyone was. Not even an introduction to 'the new guy' who would be his 'right-hand man.' And whether the new assistant needed gloves or not, he had spied those slim fingers before they disappeared into work gloves.

And Abe's face wasn't just clean-shaven – it was whiskerless. Plus, the purpose of a hat was to shove long hair out of the eyes, not off of the neck. He chuckled. Sunglasses might have helped with the deception - maybe. This woman's eyes were beautiful – no makeup required. The loose shirt was a good ploy, but men didn't have hips like that. And then there was the walk. Even loose coveralls couldn't hide that wiggle.

It took all he had not to burst out laughing when he made that crack about running around naked. Oh, if he could have seen that woman's face full on when he said it. He'd never get that chance again, but he did have the satisfaction of glimpsing her shock in the mirror. And the sight of Joe squirming. That rascal deserved it.

Well, whether the woman was competent or not, at least she was discreet about her gender and had stayed out of the way. There was nothing worse than a woman using her femininity to mother a man into getting her way. Well, unless it was using sex as a tool. Nah, being bossy and mothering were worse. At least with sex, he got a good show and a little whoopie. Then again, it usually cost him more in the end.

Yes, you made a wise decision, Joe. Hire a discreet person. Right now, I really don't give a flip about gender. As long as she can heat canned soup and bring me my liquid pain reliever on time, she can stay. Oh, and not hit every blasted pothole and curb on the way to the therapy appointments.

***

Meanwhile, in the shop

"Back to my project," Abe said. "But first things first." She reached over, swiped through the menu on the tablet, and chose Led Zeppelin. "A little mood music is in order."

Wah-ah Aaah-ah! The Immigrant Song roared through the six speakers in the rafters, energizing her and the very walls around her. She pushed the up button on the hydraulic control pendant, and the overhead hoist positioned the small side-by-side all-terrain rig where she wanted it. "Oh, what I could have created if I had one of these years ago. It's like having the Incredible Hulk at my disposal!"

The engine and drivetrain already stripped away from the John Deere's frame, she used 'The Hulk' to load the heavy golf cart batteries into the bed of the ATV. "All I need to do is fabricate a few brackets and adapters for the wheel drive motors and set them in place. A few minutes with the TIG welder to button everything together, and it's ready to shoot with primer gray. Now, what color should I paint this beautiful baby?"

***

William used his finger to swirl the half-melted ice cubes around in the glass. Joe and Abe – or whatever her real name was – hadn't even been gone five minutes and he was bored. He took his phone from his pocket and opened his email server.

"Get well, get well, get well," he read, skimming through the headings of dozens of messages. "Let's see if Joe has made it past the south gate yet."

He tapped on an icon and opened the security system. Nine camera views popped up. Before he could select the perimeter camera that covered the road leaving his property, he caught movement.

Fun movement.

William selected that camera and the small six-inch screen filled with action. A round-bottomed woman was dancing across the shop floor, wild Led Zeppelin music blaring. He started to turn down the volume on his phone but instead slid it up.

Finally, life in his life.

Whether there was any chance – or danger – of romance, there was vibrancy nearby. No one was out to see what they could get from him. No pestering him for new ideas on how to get more viewers. No requests for grants or endowments to support local charities or far-flung causes. No part of his brain, bank account, wit, wisdom, or opinion was needed with this person.

He zoomed in and looked at her project. She was tearing apart that four-wheeler Cyrus had said was the best way to get across the property. Well, best for quick trips without destroying the landscape with a monster truck. She was skilled, too. She was handling that impact wrench like an artist with a paintbrush.

And there, in a heap on the floor next to it. "Well, I'll be damned. She's stripped the hub motors out of that golf cart I had sent in. Cyrus said it wouldn't work, but it looks like she's going to at least try."

William sat in the game room until he realized how uncomfortable he was. He picked up his glass to finish his drink before moving to the recliner and noticed the ice had completely melted. He swilled it back and set the tumbler down. "Dinner, drinks, and a show. I can finish the entertainment in my room. I don't care what time the clock shows, it's been a long day."

He huffed and added. "A long week. Hell, a long life!"

***

Abe danced while she wrenched or torched parts from both rigs, singing as she made her way through phase one of the customization conversion. "Heaven's a shop full of tools and impossible projects to bring into existence!"

Watching on the smartphone app from his room, William commented, "Only if you're very clever."

Stunned that he'd made the remark out loud, he remembered he hadn't enabled the walkie-talkie function. She hadn't heard him.

"Pervert," he scolded himself. "Let her create in peace. After all, you already know she's motivated. Shut off your peephole and go to sleep. She's sure to show you the conversion eventually."

Using the cane hanging from the back of the wheelchair, he pushed off his loafers. "Pretty handy multitool. I'll bet it's even a good backscratcher." He swung it over his shoulder to test his theory. "Yup. That's three uses. Care to try for four?"

After a few minutes in the bathroom, he was stripped and ready for bed. "Four, five, six, seven," he counted, recalling how many times he'd used his diamond willow cane. "I guess flipping up the toilet seat counts as a function, too."

He used the polished antler handle to pull down the bedspread. "Eight," and wiggled his way under the covers. He set the cane in the middle of the bed, then realized he hadn't shut off the light. "Nine," he said, using the tip to click the switch on the base of the lamp. "We'll make it to double digits tomorrow, I'm sure."

***

It was midnight before Abe ran out of steam. "Oh, crap. That's right. I have to take the old fart to town tomorrow. Oh, well. At least it isn't until after lunch. I can squeeze in another hour or two."

Deciding to install the bracket she'd just cut out of plate steel, she picked it up without thinking – and without gloves.

"Shit!" she yelled, dropping it to the floor.

With her one good hand, Abe fumbled and got the lid off her water bottle. She stuck her burned thumb and two fingers into the narrow opening, tipping the bottle to give them an icy bath.

"Aahh." She plopped down on the shop stool and let her shoulders slump against the newly plastered wall, willing the throbbing burn to go away. As soon as she pulled her hand out, the air hit the newly formed blisters and she yelped.

"Okay. That's it. I'm going to bed. Fatigue is probably the number one cause of shop injuries. My unfinished mess will still be waiting for me in the morning. The first thing I'm going to do when I get back is to find a pair of flexible welding gloves. One size does *not* fit all." She chuffed. "Yeah, and none of them work if you don't wear them at all, idiot."

Abe's mood brightened when she walked into her apartment. The aroma of fresh ground Arabica lingered from when she had set up the coffee maker earlier. She shucked off her clothes and went into the kitchen. Pulling off a long length of paper towel, she awkwardly folded it and wrapped it around her burned fingers. She quickly ran the impromptu bandaged hand under cold tap water, squeezed out the excess water, and headed to bed.

Pausing in the living room, she looked out the huge picture window at the moon over the hills. "Who puts such a magnificent view over a shop?" She chuckled. "Who cares? It's mine now, or at least it is for as long as I have this job. Here's hoping the old fart doesn't find out I'm a woman. Or at least, doesn't get royally pissed when he does find out. It's going to take a long time for me to get tired of this place."

Abe fell into a deep sleep, her cool, damp paper towel-wrapped hand snuggled close to her chest. When she awoke to the smell of her freshly brewed coffee, she was unusually stiff. "Oh, that's why. I don't think I even turned over once."

Stretching luxuriously in the high-count Egyptian cotton sheets, she sighed. "What did I do to deserve this?" She slumped, remembering her upcoming duties. "Or what do I have to do to keep this?"

Brnnggg! Brnngg!

Abe answered the phone on the kitchen counter.

"Good morning, Agatha…I mean, Abe," Joe said, chuckling softly.

"You know, I wouldn't mind you using my given name so much if I didn't believe you only did it to anger me, Joe-Suff. By the way, is Suff short for Insufferable?"

"No, I just can't think of you as an Abe." He chuckled. "Well, I have to admit that irritating you is a little bit of fun. I guess I missed out, not having any siblings. I can't tease my wife, or she'd never sleep with me again."

"Well, you definitely won't have that problem with me since I never slept with you in the past and have no plans for it in the future. So, why did you call me so bright and early?"

"Oh, shoot. That's right: time zone difference. Sorry about that. I just wanted to find out how the first night went. Did you fix him dinner? Did he find out you're a woman? If so, did he blow a gasket?"

"Slow down, Joe. I just woke up." Abe held the phone out with one hand and stretched, not stifling her lung-clearing yawn. She filled up the cup from the bathroom sink and took a quick drink of water, ignoring the minor throb of her blistered fingers, before she lay back in bed.

"Okay, now I can think. Let's see. No, no, and no."

"What?"

"You asked me three questions and I gave you three answers. No, I didn't fix dinner for either of us, no he didn't find out I was a woman, so no, he didn't blow a gasket. Actually, you saw him last, not me. I went to the shop before you left, remember? I assume he's still alive and happy. I haven't heard him complaining about anything or asking for his morning coffee."

"Or whisky," Joe added. "Please, take care of him. Or at least don't let him harm himself. Good business partners are hard to find, even if they're grumpy and tend to drink too much. Put on your androgynous garb and pop in to check on him. Maybe offer him a cup of coffee or toaster pastry. I'd do it myself but..."

"But that's not in your skill set, right?"

"Well, yes. Sort of. But Abe, you don't have to do much beyond making sure he gets to his physical therapy appointments."

"Or find out I'm a woman."

"Well, I kind of feel bad about that. I don't know whether he would care about it or not."

"What? Then why the big deception?"

"Well, just in case. Besides, Dorothy really wanted you to be in a better place, have a better shot at a good life."

"Shoot, Joe. If I'd known you two had thrown a pity party for me, I wouldn't be here. I can take care of myself."

"We know you can, but you deserve better than living in a rusty tin can in the swamp, tuning up lawnmowers, and turning in pop bottles to buy food. Besides, you're the most creative person I know when it comes to mechanical challenges. If I put a man in there to work with William, the two would probably kill each other."

"So, what you're saying is he doesn't play well with others?"

"No, not really. Well, not too well. Hell, that really doesn't matter. He's interested in mechanical projects and cars, but he's not a mechanic. Plus, I know if I were wounded, I'd rather have a member of the opposite sex take care of me. I guess I figured it would be the same for him."

Abe ran the fingers of her uninjured hand through her hair and realized she was nude, in bed, in another man's home – or at least in an apartment on his vast estate. Suddenly, she felt naked and vulnerable. She pulled the bedsheet close.

"Hey, Joe. I need to cut this short and get the day started. I'll make sure he has food and booze available, and that he makes it to his PT appointments. That's it, right?"

"Yes, but I've hidden all the booze. The list of where the bottles are is taped under the fax phone on your kitchen counter. You know, the machine you use to send in your grocery list. Don't let him have more than two bottles a day."

"Got it." She hung up the phone and shuddered.

What had she gotten herself into?

***

William rolled over onto his repaired shoulder and shot upright in pain. "Bloody hell," he began, then bit his bottom lip and stifled his curses, remembering the words of the old man he'd met in the hospital.

Dressed in oversized scrubs with a borrowed stethoscope draped around his neck, the avid fan had made it past security pretending to be a medic. "Your body will heal faster with peace than anger. Surround yourself with beauty and gentle words. Allow the bones to knit and the muscles and ligaments to come together again with the harmony of love that was their beginning."

The old man's soft touch as he spoke those mystical words truly eased William's shoulder pain. Just recalling that moment of magic helped. Now he was glad he had sent the guru with the colorful braided bracelet away with a heartfelt thank you and had his assistant send him an autographed book.

Still in bed, William leaned forward, scooting and twisting until his feet hung over the edge. "Easy does it," he told his body, readying himself. "You can do it."

As soon as he put his hand down to assist in the butt lift, pain shot up his arm, and he collapsed backward. "Bloody hell..."

Ping.

William froze at the unfamiliar sound. Did something in his body break? He grinned despite the pain when he realized what it was. The proximity alert in the shop had been tripped. The clever female fabricator was back. What wonders would she create today?

Inspired by curiosity rather than frustrated by pain and feelings of helplessness, William managed to get himself dressed without one swear word. "Shoehorn – use number ten." He pulled the bedroom door open further. "What the heck. Let's call that one eleven even if I turned the knob and got it started without the cane."

The aroma of fresh coffee wafted in from the kitchen. "Liquid motivation." He began his wheelchair ride down the hall, using his cane like an oar, 'rowing' his way to breakfast with the cane's tip pushing against the floor. "Twelve."

The coffee maker espresso combination was sitting on the counter, a full pot of brewed coffee calling to him. In front of it was a large, polished aluminum thermal mug with a sheet of paper beneath it. 'Sorry, I don't know how to make the fancy stuff. Toaster pastries are in the bread box, frozen breakfast sandwiches on the middle shelf of the freezer. Ring the shop if you need help. Abe.'

"Nice blocky letters. No flourish or little hearts. Written on a piece of fax paper, not girly stationery. Hmm. If I didn't know better, I wouldn't know better." He chuckled to himself. "This is going to be fun. Who's going to slip up first?"

***

Abe dug through the shop supplies cabinet and found a pair of barbecue grilling gloves. She bit the manufacturer's tag off and tossed it in the trash. "Not welding gloves but rated good enough for what I need them for."

She threw the cooled steel blanks she had cut into a wire hot-tank basket along with a few of the other pieces that needed to be machined. "What am I forgetting?" She rolled her shoulders, uneasy. "Something's not right..." A set of vice grips fell to the floor and clanged.

"That's it! Music!"

Back to the digital display on the tablet, she swiped down, chose her tunes, then stepped back and let loose.

"Bicycle! Bicycle! I want to ride my bicycle!" she sang with the music, her energy level tripled with the Queen classic. "I want to ride my bike..."

She worked with passion, occasionally consulting her notes, but she knew her design by heart. It was as if everything had fallen into place like a giant jigsaw puzzle when Cyrus told her what was there to work with. She nodded and pretended to agree as he explained how he would do it, but as soon as he was gone, so was his concept.

She was experienced with re-powering motor vehicles and apparently, he wasn't. She'd done something similar with a go-cart for her neighbor's daughter the year before. The converted electric dump cart had taken first place for originality, but only third at the finish line. This time, though, she had more powerful batteries and better wheels and tires.

Work on the project and the time went quickly, the playlist reloading twice. Suddenly, a loud voice boomed from the walls. "We'd better go now, or we'll be late for the appointment."

Clank! Clatter, clatter.

Tools and hardware fell to the floor as she spun around, looking for the source of the noise.

"I'll meet you at the car."

"Shit," she huffed, then looked at the clock. "Be right there."

Abe quickly shucked her coveralls and grabbed her loose denim shirt, putting it on as she shut the door behind her. All she could think of was whether she had the keys or not and if the intercom from the house to the shop also had video capabilities.

She stopped running when she saw William was already in the backseat of the car, eyes forward, jaw set.

"Location is already programmed in the GPS and the keys are in the ignition."

Head down, she grunted, "Thanks," hoping he hadn't heard the squeak as she dropped her voice an octave lower. She climbed in, put on the seatbelt, and sighed in frustration. He'd been in the front seat to set the GPS. She reached over and pressed the button, returning the seat to driver two position. Resisting the urge to ask if the temperature was okay or how he was feeling, she drove in absolute silence.

And discomfort.

The second tall cup of coffee she'd drunk wasn't just sneaking up on her, it was attacking her with full-blown misery. The more she tried not to think about it, the worse it was. A cold sweat broke out, her head started spinning, and she was afraid she was going to pass out.

"I know we're running close on time," she said, "but I have to make a pit stop. Now."

"Do what you have to do." William heard the smile in his own voice and was sure she could, too.

A sharp turn down a county road just far enough to be off the highway was good enough for Abe. She put the Cadillac in park, left the motor running, and rushed to the front of the car. She quickly dropped her jeans and squatted in front of the radiator. She knew she was out of his sight, but she was unabashedly showing her bare ass to hawks, coyotes, or any oncoming traffic.

When she came back to the car, William tipped his head in acknowledgment. One hand covered his face as if deep in thought. Or maybe he was trying to keep from laughing out loud or making a snarky comment.

William's jaws hurt from holding back the wide grin. 'What? Bashful, are you?' 'Can't hold your coffee anymore?' 'Too good for indoor plumbing?' Each thought and smart-aleck remark that crossed his mind made it tougher to keep a straight face. Failing to do so completely, he looked down and hid the smirk behind his hand.

Abe scratched the top of her head as she climbed in, hiding her fiery blush. No, it wasn't the color she was hiding. It was the tears that were trying to leak out. Well, whether he knew she was a woman or not, she'd learned something very interesting about him. He was a gentleman.

At least until – or if – he made a crude remark about her being bashful. Or having a weak bladder. Or afraid of public restrooms.

Despite the quick stop, they arrived at the physical therapist's appointment five minutes early. She hopped out and opened his door, then ran around back to get the wheelchair. Only it wasn't there.

"I thought…" she began, then realized she was using her own

voice.

"I'll tell you what," William said. "I'll see if I can make it in if you spot me." He winked in a mischievous, non-sexist way. "Just in case I fall, you run in front of me, so I have something soft to land on."

She replied with a chuckle. "Or I can borrow one from the clinic. I really am sorry I got carried away in the shop. I totally lost track of time."

"Don't worry about that. I *will* let you take that wheelchair from that gentleman there, though. It looks like he's ready to have a coronary, seeing me ready to walk in under my own power."

Abe took the wheelchair from the excited aide. "I got this," she said.

"But...but..." the man in his late twenties said, suddenly disappointed. "I wanted to take him in."

Abe looked at him and squinted. "Don't worry. You won't lose your job. It's my job, too, to take care of him."

"Lucky," the man said softly and walked away.

"Wha..." Abe shook her head as she positioned the chair beside William and set the brakes. "Ready?"

"As I'll ever be." William settled into the chair and looked up at her, seeing her face for the first time. Her features were pleasant and unpainted. Although lightly lined with years, she radiated a healthy glow.

"Sorry if I'm staring," he said. "It's just you're so...so...vibrant."

"Wow. Thanks, but I think that's because I don't have to pee anymore."

William laughed out loud and shook his head. "Well, let's hope that's the cure for old age, aches, and pains. If this place is anything like that hospital I was in, it'll be a while before I'm laughing again."

She patted him on his uninjured shoulder. "Not if I can help it. I have a few old elephant jokes that need a new audience."

"What you really need are some *new* elephant jokes for an *old* audience. I think I've either heard or shared every elephant joke ever told."

50

As Abe wheeled William into the building, heads turned and fingers pointed, whispers and a few 'Hey, theres!' called out.

"Am I missing something?" she asked William.

"Nope," he said and bit his bottom lip.

Even in the pucker brush of Montana, his face was known. Of course, it was. Thirteen seasons of their automobile and extreme adventure shows produced overseas were now in worldwide syndication. The miracle wasn't that this whole town knew him, but that his caretaker didn't.

***

"Forget what I said," he groaned as Abe tried to help him out of the car. "I don't want to laugh. They hurt me so bad in there, I'll never recover. I want to bathe in liquor. Drink it for breakfast, lunch, and dinner."

Abe clenched her jaws as she tried to hoist his rigid, unresponsive bulk toward the seat. "Can't you help me just a little?"

William lifted one leg then yelped. "Noo. Damn! Right now, I'd even let you stick me with a blunt fuel line to give me an IV of whatever poison there's left in that liquor cabinet."

"Yeah, well, poison is what it is. Or was. It's empty. Not even a dribble of alcohol." She lifted his arm and wedged under his shoulder. After a deep breath of fortitude and mumbled curse words, she managed to transfer him into the wheelchair.

"And I'm not yours or anyone else's doctor. Giving you 'personal' attention isn't part of my job description. However, from my own experience, I can tell you that an Epsom salts bath will take away your body aches and pains more than swilling alcohol will. I'll prepare one for you and even help you get into the tub before I let you have more of those dehydrating toxins."

"Hmph!" William's former flowery outlook on healing had disappeared and a black mold of disgust had replaced it. "Just get me booze. Lots and lots of booze."

"No."

"What? You can't tell me no."

"Okay, then I'll tell you, 'Bullshit.'"

"Where do you get off talking to me like that? Don't you know who signs your paychecks?"

Abe laughed. "Actually, I do, and it's not you."

She pushed the wheelchair over the threshold into the house and positioned him opposite a Chippendale chair. With a dramatic flair that was her personal ploy to work up nerve, she sat down, placed her elbows on her knees, and leaned forward.

"Joseph Edward Patterson hired me. He signs my checks. He has informed me that you are to get no more than one bottle of booze a day," she fibbed. "I am to keep you from harming yourself, feed you – or at least offer food to you – and make sure you go to your physical therapist appointments. Oh, and if you do manage to hurt yourself with your stubbornness or stupidity, I will make sure you get medical attention."

"You're nothing but a bitchy old maid on a power trip because you can get around and I can't."

Abe nodded in agreement, her shock at his bluntness turning into glee. "You're right on most parts. I'm a bitchy old maid who can get around and you can't. But I'm not on a power trip."

"Then why did you pretend to be a man?"

"What?" She sat up and pulled her shoulders back. "I never pretended to be a man."

"Yes, you did."

Abe noticed William was sitting up straighter now, his discomfort forgotten with the adrenaline from an old-fashioned couple's argument. She jumped back in, not holding back her indignation.

"I didn't reveal my femininity because this job position was biased toward a male employee. Believe it or not, Joe thought I was the best person for the job. But..." She held one finger up, "he thought you wouldn't allow a woman padding around your domain. He didn't want me to lose out on employment because I didn't have a cock." She paused and added, "Not that one was needed for the job."

William glared at her as she gave her recitation, his mouth twitching at the word cock and returning to a straight line of grimness when she was done. His eyes, however, couldn't hide his mirth.

"What?" she asked.

"I didn't say anything," William said without emotion.

"I'm a woman, I speak body language fluently."

William swallowed hard and let loose the grin he'd been holding back. "All right. Sorry. I just couldn't help imagining what part of your brief job description required male genitalia."

Her scowl softened, and soon both were chuckling. "I guess we'll never find out," she said.

"You wrestled me out of the car well enough. You're stronger than many men and probably gentler in getting me out in one piece. At least, no new broken bones. I still want a drink, though."

"I'll get you a cup of soup first, then make the call. Joe and his Father Goose ploy with hiding the booze is a pain." She shrugged. "But, I'll put in a good word for you. I'll at least tell him you made it to and from the appointment. Now, whether you can manage to do your daily at-home exercises remains to be seen. That might be worth a second bottle if you do."

William chuckled as Abe stood up, then stopped, the laugh stuck in his throat. The top button of her shirt had come undone while maneuvering him out of the backseat. Buxom cleavage was visible, tantalizing but not obscene. He turned away. "Don't bother with preparing soup. Just make the call and find out where he hid the whisky."

Noticing his change in tone and focus, Abe looked down and saw the popped button. Rather than fix it, she rolled her shoulders – shifting her shirt so her décolletage wasn't visible – and continued as if nothing had happened. "I can make the call while microwaving a light supper. It's no bother and part of my job."

William felt a smirk arise.

"And yes," she said in reply to his unspoken remark. "No cock required for either one of those tasks."

Chapter 5

Late-breaking news item. One more person has been added to the thousands around the world looking for automobile enthusiast and TV star William Gagnant. Eddie 'Razor' Rizzo has escaped from the Greater Queens Mental Health Facility. Three weeks ago, Razor broke into the Plaza Hotel room of William Gagnant. He was apprehended with the star's socks, underwear, and other personal items. Rather than have him arrested for the theft, Mr. Gagnant asked that Rizzo be held for a thorough psychiatric assessment. Rizzo escaped with only two days left on his mandated evaluation. The vehicle he fled in belonged to one of the employees at the facility. The owner said no charges will be filed if the car is returned in its original condition.

***

Abe dashed into the kitchen. As soon as she was out of William's sight, she refastened her buttons. She grabbed one of the cans with a red label from the pantry shelf, popped off the lid, and dumped it into an oversized soup mug. Her nose wrinkled at the musky scent. She looked in the cup. The contents looked like a muddy puddle with rusty bits and clumps of orange fat floating on top. She checked the label again. It wasn't the chunky soup she thought she'd chosen but chili con carne.

"Damn. Not exactly an Englishman's comfort food. Well, here's hoping he likes Texican slop with beans because that's what he's getting tonight. If not, he can go hungry."

While dinner was heating in the microwave, Abe made her status update phone call.

"Hey, Joe... Yeah, well, we made it to and from his physical therapy appointment today. Actually, I was tempted to leave the ornery so-and-so at the clinic. He wasn't too bad going in, but the yelps coming from him when those therapists were working him over... Whoo boy. No, he didn't hit anyone. He actually kept his curse words down to PG13 level… Oh, you are? I'm sorry. Call me back when you're done. Tell Dorothy I said hi. And *bon appétit* to you both."

Abe hung up and watched the ceramic cup go around in the microwave, bubbling and sputtering. Just like the stinky mess she was heating, her life was going around and around, getting nowhere. But she could walk, cook, and pull wrenches without any problems. She suddenly felt sorry for William and his lack of control over his life.

"He can't even zap a can of chili. Well, it's not my job to cook gourmet meals for him but it might brighten his mood if I spruce this up. I know I'd appreciate it if someone did that for me."

Abe found several bags of salad components in the vegetable drawer of the refrigerator. She poured some of them into fluted glass custard cups. "Chopped green onions, a sprinkle of shredded cheddar, and a plop of diced tomatoes. Not bad." She added a dollop of sour cream into a fourth bowl and created instant garnishes. A smartly folded fabric napkin and a tumbler of ice on a silver serving platter completed her task.

"Much better. Colorful condiments well-presented with glass and silver, and even a two-dollar can of pintos, red sauce, and unrecognizable minced meat can look like a first-class meal."

Checking to make sure all blouse closures were secure, Abe entered the room with a smile of accomplishment. She'd created a beautiful dinner in under five minutes for the master of the house, even if it was basically spiced dog food.

Eyes closed in pain, William lifted his face when he heard her enter the room. "What's that and do you expect me to eat it in here?"

"It's your dinner and you can dine in any room you'd like or even outside. I'm only going to move it once, so make up your mind. I have other projects to attend to."

"So, I'm a project?"

"No, you're a job. I'm just here to offer you food, keep you safe, and ensure you make it to medical and therapeutic appointments, remember? Coddling you was actually discouraged."

William started to insist she move him into the dining room then eyed the empty liquor cabinet across the hall. "Just roll me into the game room and hand me the remote. I'll drink my dinner in there."

"No."

"No? Which one, 'No'?"

"No, you're not going to drink your dinner because I haven't been able to get through to Joe to find out whether you've earned a bottle of whisky or not."

Joe lunged forward, grasping the arms of the wheelchair, lifting himself so high, he was almost standing. "Joe is not the one to decide whether I can drink or not," he barked. "I made the decision to use alcohol – not those habit-forming opioids – to numb the pain. Now, dammit, bring me my meds!"

Abe marched across the hall and slammed the dinner tray on the bar counter. With as much ire as William had shown, she grabbed his walker and set it down forcefully in front of him. Steely eyes of gray ablaze, she glared at him, daring him to speak, then stepped behind the bar and grabbed the bottle of whisky she had found hidden in an ice bucket. She slammed it down on the tray, rattling the dishes, jostling the ice in the glass tumbler.

"If you want it so bad, walk over here and get it. It's your choice whether you eat first, or drink on an empty stomach and burn a hole in your gut. You have to pour it for yourself. I may be your 'drug pusher' and cook, but I'm not your cocktail waitress."

"Damned poor cook," William mumbled as he grasped the walker, struggling to stand up.

"What did you say?" Abe bellowed although she had heard him clearly enough.

He took a deep breath then forced his elbows straight and stood upright. Avoiding her eyes, he concentrated on each step until he made it to the bar. One arm on the bolstered counter for support, he turned and settled onto the leather barstool. "It wasn't important. Go take care of your 'other' projects."

Biting off the words, "I don't need your permission," Abe strode away from the bar toward the door. She heard him mumble again, this time not understanding. "If you have something to say to me, speak up!" she growled.

William cleared his throat and swallowed, his nose wrinkled in disgust at the pungency of the red chili and cumin. He blinked at the food. "It may smell like dog food, but it looks nice. Thank you."

"Yeah, well, you had a rough day."

William lifted his chin and watched as she left.

Shoulders back with pride, this woman was tough.

She also had the roundest ass and the cutest wiggle he'd ever seen.

"Oh, Lord. Why did You send someone like her into my life when I can't even walk? Hmph! Okay, I get it. You sent me motivation. Well, all I can say is You sent a hell of a carrot to this old jackass. You definitely got my attention."

William leaned closer to the food and sniffed the brown goo in the bowl. "Mercy! Nothing could help that mess." He put the ice bucket lid over it and started opening cabinet doors. "*Voila!* Tortilla chips. *Canapés mexicains* washed down with Scottish whisky on American soil. A fine international meal."

***

Abe watched as a dusty, blue Ford Focus slowly approached the front of the house, rolling to a stop in front of her. Two young men in tee shirts and torn jeans, their looks as different as surfers and grunge musicians, stepped out. "May I help you?" she asked.

"Um, yeah," the blond with the red Ford ball cap said. "We wanted to know if we were at the right place. I mean… Does William Gagnant live here? We were hoping to meet him. We're his biggest fans."

His dark-haired buddy stepped in front of him and took over the conversation. He winked at her and looked her up and down, licking his bottom lip. "Yeah, we came all the way from New York to see if we could get his autograph."

Disgusted by the thinly veiled flirt from a man half her age, Abe still felt she had to be courteous. Joe had said something about wanting to keep William's recovery location discreet. Apparently, William was

58

famous. If that was so, she didn't want to alienate any of his fans. *He didn't look like an actor. Could he be an author? He must be because these two were definitely stalkers.*

"I'm sorry guys. I'm afraid you've come a long way for nothing." *Cool. No committal on whether William lived here or not. Keep the grump safe and her job secure.*

"Can we look around, though?" Flirty asked.

"Why?" Abe's fingers twitched, wishing they were wrapped around a crescent wrench.

"Why not?"

"Because it's private property, that's why. You haven't been invited here, but now I am *un-inviting* you. Please leave."

"Come on," Ford cap said, gently pulling on his cohort's elbow. "Maybe that guy at the clinic gave you the wrong address."

"Yeah, so let's go get my fifty bucks back from him. That was my lunch money."

"Sorry to have disturbed you, ma'am," the blond said, tipping his hat. "Have a good day."

Abe stood her ground, her back to the upright gatepost, making sure they left. Flirty got behind the wheel of the flashy car and ball-cap guy took one more look around the property before getting in. The dark-haired driver gunned the engine, then looked at her with disgust rather than lust. He dropped the transmission into gear and peeled out, rear tires spinning in place before lurching forward, smearing black tread marks against the sand-colored cobblestones.

"That was weird. William must be a Stephen King league author to have such a dedicated fan base. Who would have thought it?"

Abe heard the phone ring and sprinted to the shop to answer it. She picked up the receiver and blurted, "Hello? Hello? Are you still there?"

"I got you a cell phone in case you were away from the house," Joe said without answering her question. "Why don't you carry it with you? No, no; never mind. I just wanted to give you a heads up. Life's going to be changing for you pretty soon."

"You aren't going to tell me William has a twin who's hurt and on the way, too, are you? I don't think I could handle that, no matter how much I love this place."

"No, no. The truck is on its way there. It has your motorcycle and the surprise project I mentioned on it. But before we talk about that, tell me more about your trip to the physical therapist."

Abe pulled up a shop stool and sat down. "Well, as I said before, we made it in and out of the appointment without him injuring himself or anyone else. Getting him out of the car here – after all the stretching and pulling or whatever torture they put him through – was a battle of wits, words, and worn-out bodies. I swear, I think I wrenched every one of my tug-of-war muscles."

Abe rolled her shoulder, suddenly aware of how sore she was from the effort, and continued. "I just served Sir Grumps-a-lot a late lunch but whether he eats it or just sticks to drinking his pain medicine isn't up to me. And no, I wasn't going to hang around and find out. He's a grown man and can make his own decisions about what he puts in his body. Don't worry, though. I won't let him hurt himself. I remember you said no more than two bottles of booze a day. He's just now starting on the first one. That should keep him out of my hair. And I'm almost done with that electric ATV conversion you and Cyrus talked me into. You'll be able to sneak up on rattlesnakes after I'm done with this stealthy little side-by-side."

Abe turned around on the stool and cozied up against the wall. "So, do you have an idea when that truck will be here? And what's my surprise? No fair saying if you told me, then it wouldn't be a surprise. I'd rather be prepared than shocked."

Joe chuckled. Abe sounded a lot like his wife. They both loved surprises but didn't want to be surprised. "The email update I just received said two hours or so. The 'optional project' is in a couple of crates. You'll need to find room for them. I don't want to tell you too much but I will say that one contains a mostly wrecked vehicle and the other has repair parts for same. William said he didn't want anything to do with it, but I had to move it somewhere. Since it is legally his and I don't have the right to sell it, I decided to send it there. You don't have to take this on, but if you're bored, it can be your next project."

"As long as it isn't a lawnmower or golf cart, I'm good." Abe paused and added, "It isn't a chain saw, is it? I've rebuilt or repaired enough of those to last two lifetimes."

"No, I said it was a vehicle. How about a first-year-of-issue pony, built by Ford," Joe teased.

"A sixty-four Mustang? You're kidding me. Rebuild it if I want? Hell yeah! It's coming here at the same time as my Norton? I won't know what to do first: ride my baby or put that pony back together again. Oh, you are so trying to get me to stick around here for more than a month. And before you ask, the four-legged mustangs are fine. I found where the oats were kept. I'll sprinkle a few cups on the other side of the fence to attract them. I'll also make sure the water trough is clean. That ought to bring them in for dessert and drinks. I'll get a live show and friendly company."

"Still not a fan of movies, eh?"

"You know me, Joe. It's been years since I watched TV or even went to a movie theater. Nope, nothing in them I care about. I know my way around a library, although I haven't had the chance to go to the one here. I'm kind of curious now about what kind of books William writes. Yeah, I figured out that's what he does. A couple of his fans dropped by, but I shooed them away without letting them know this was his place.

"Hey, unless you have something else, I'll sign off. I need to rearrange my workspace to make room for my red, white, and blue two-wheeler and my new four-wheeled project. Oh, and thank you very much for the job, Joe. By bringing in a '64 Mustang for me to rebuild and my '76 Norton to ride, I've gone from really liking this place to positively loving it."

"Uh, great. I'm glad it's all working out. William really is a great guy, too. Just think of how you'd feel if your places were reversed – you were the one all banged up and he was tending to you. Remember, when he's cranky, it's because he's hurting."

"Right... See ya later. And give Dorothy a big hug and a squeeze for me."

"Goodbye." Joe hung up the phone, confused. "She thinks William's an author? And fans came out to see him? Sounds like there are at least two loose lips in the system.

***

"I think I'm ready for a little Alice Cooper therapy." Abe picked up the digital tablet and scrolled through the playlists. "Ah. Here we go." She hit select all and volume up, then stepped back.

The heavy metal song blasted through the speakers, further invigorating the already excited woman. "It ain't the way…" she sang along, dancing as she worked, shoving toolboxes and anything else on casters. She grabbed the pallet jack and slid up to it like it was a dance pole, slithering up and down the handle, ending with a hipshot flourish. Soon, cases of oils, shop towels, and miscellaneous supplies were moved to an unused corner, Abe bumping and grinding her way to a ballroom-sized work area.

She unplugged the modified ATV four-wheeler and sat in it. "One last test drive before I sign off on you. Here we go."

She hit the remote and opened the shop overhead door. Out she went, a bucket of sweetened oats loaded in the back. "Let's bring a banquet to the girls tonight, shall we?"

Small rocks and pebbles flung aside, branches cracked and leaves wrinkled like cellophane as Abe drove to the ravine. She pulled up alongside the sturdy plastic trough and called out, "Care for dessert first tonight, girls?"

Startled, the mares ran away but stopped after a few yards. Curious, they slowed and turned around, their noses twitching at the smell of their familiar treat in an unfamiliar place. Abe poured out several piles of the sweetened oats near the salt lick and went back to sit in the cart, silent as a gentle breeze.

The horses' bewilderment was soon overcome by desire for the calorie-rich treat. The harem plodded slowly toward it, unsure of the new intruder but comfortable with the new person.

When they were finished, Abe said, "Thanks for the show. See you tomorrow," and drove away silently, glad the peace of the moment wasn't being spoiled by the noise of a four-stroke engine or the stink of gasoline exhaust.

"That went well," she said when she pulled into the shop. "As long as I keep the battery cables disconnected, the charge will hold." She took a black marker out of her shirt pocket and squatted beside the rear wheel on the driver's side. 'ABE 2021' she wrote in two-inch tall blocky letters.

"Signed off and ready for my next project."

***

William finished his light meal while watching Abe chat on the phone, frustrated that he could only catch snatches of her conversation because she was too close to the wall. Something she had heard, though, really excited her. She cranked up her tunes and was dancing like a strip club dancer as she shuffled boxes around, creating an open space big enough for a ballroom floor.

A pause in the action came when she went out of sight. A half-hour later, she was back, driving the now electric-powered side-by-side four-wheeler. The older John Deere rig had come with the property. 'Perfect for checking out the wildlife,' Joe had told him.

"Perfect for scaring them away," William mumbled, grabbing the whisky bottle Abe had let him have as his evening medicine. He held it up and checked how much he'd drunk. Not much.

William chuckled at himself. "You're not *that* old if you'd rather watch a woman's moves than drink hard liquor, no matter how much you hurt." He dumped a generous splash over the little bit of ice that was left in the glass. "But what woman in the world would want a busted-up old man like me unless it was for money or fame?"

Chapter 6

Controversy on the freedom of the press front. On entry, fans who attended the now infamous Mesa Verde Speedway revival were required to sign a waiver saying they would not record the event. Several poor-quality copies of the fiery rollover crash in which fan favorite William Gagnant was rescued by an unidentified – and supposedly supernatural being – have shown up on YouTube. The heavily sponsored videos are purportedly earning millions. Joseph Patterson, the CEO of Fast Dudes Enterprises and producer of the popular AROUND THE WORLD IN 80 CARS franchise, said all video and audio recordings of the event are the property of FDE per the signed agreements. A freeze has been put on all monies earned from the videos until the case can be heard by the courts.

***

Beep... Beep... Beep...

The familiar slow and steady chime of a backup alarm cut through the shouts of Alice Cooper's School's Out. Abe quickly silenced her tunes and ran outside to greet the truck.

"This door," she said, guiding the semi-tractor toward the bay with the newly cleared work area.

Not willing to sit still and have him do all the work, Abe assisted in the unloading. After a few minutes of maneuvering with the liftgate and two tfloor jacks, all three crates were inside, the job complete. The truck driver handed her the papers to sign. While her head was down, reading what she was signing, he checked her out.

"Just wondering," the man said, "Is it true *he* lives here?"

She chuckled, remembering the two young visitors who had shown up earlier. She handed back the clipboard and paperwork. "Well, all I'll tell you is that a *he* does live here. I'm not at liberty to tell you which *he* he is, though."

"Well, if *he* is the *he*, tell him I'm one of his biggest fans."

Abe nodded and winked with a glint of mischief in her eye. "Will do…but only if *he* is the *he.*"

The driver took his manifest and climbed into the cab of his truck, as unsure as ever if this really was the home of one of the stars of *Around the World in Eighty Cars.* "If this is his place, I sure like the looks of his mechanic. Wow!"

Abe pushed the button and down came the ten-foot-tall shop door, shutting out daylight and distractions. "Let's see what we have here…"

Crowbar in hand, she pulled boards off the crates. The first one exposed a stack of nested body parts and cartons. She stopped at the second one: a charred and contorted mass of metal that had once been a car.

"What in the hell? Oh, my goodness. This must be what William was in when he crashed. And he walked away from it? That had to be some sort of miracle."

She lifted and pushed pieces around, looking under bent fenders, wrinkling her nose at the stench of charred wiring harnesses and hoses. "And it's going to take another miracle to put this thing back together again, even with new parts. The only thing salvageable – I hope – is the serial number plate."

Abe finally stopped investigating the remains of the disaster and washed her hands. "It's too quiet in here. I'm not ready for rock and roll, though. I feel as if I'm getting ready to tell a patient some bad news." She selected ambient ocean sounds, too somber with the physical remains of a man's near-death to enjoy upbeat music.

"Well, at least I know what's in this one," she said, pulling off the planks of wood from the end of the taller crate, exposing her patriotic color-themed motorcycle. "You're just as sweet as ever, my Snortin' Norton. Care to go for a ride while the sun still shines?"

She looked up at the clock and saw it was already eight o'clock. "Shit! I should have made him at least a light snack for dinner."

Leaving the crowbar on the ground, she rushed outside, half-running into the house. She checked the game room. Empty. The kitchen and living room. Empty. Just as she was getting ready to call out and ask if he needed anything, she heard his bedroom door open.

"Come to see if I was still alive?" he asked.

A flush of embarrassment washed over her along with a sense of relief. "You're too ornery to die," she said with a nervous chuckle. "Checking up on you is part of my job, though. However, since I was never given a schedule…"

"Now is as good a time as any, right?" William countered, trying to contain a grin.

"If you're hungry, I can scare up something." She turned and headed toward the kitchen, not waiting for an answer.

"As long as it's not brown," he called out after her.

She stopped and looked back, one eyebrow raised.

He came her way, clutching the walker and setting it down in front of him as he made his way down the broad hall. "That brown mass in a mug you served me. I have to ask, would you have eaten that?"

"Honestly? No. I would have eaten the garnishes instead. I'm truly sorry. I was in a hurry. I thought I had grabbed a soup or stew."

"Well, we think alike there. I did eat those brilliant sides with some chips. Come on. Let's go see what's in the kitchen. Maybe I can help."

She paced him as they walked through the huge room. "A man in a kitchen? How novel."

"Some of the greatest chefs in the world are men," he said.

"Only because they just recently started letting women into culinary schools. Julia Child had a heck of a time getting in." She grabbed two boxes of apple juice from the cabinet and set them on the counter. With the practice of many years, she quickly pulled off the plastic wrappers and stabbed the straws into the tops. "Here."

"Thanks. Well, hopefully access to education isn't as difficult these days. There's a lot of worth in a woman. They can do pretty much anything a man can if given the right tools and instructions."

"Yes, but there's a lot to overcome when it comes to tradition. For generations, all men wanted was a woman to cook and clean for them, make beer runs, and be on standby for a convenient romp in the sack when the urge hit. Never mind her needs. A woman was supposed to be content knowing she'd kept her husband supplied with hot cooked meals and another generation to carry on the family name. Yeah, even if that surname was something as boring as Smith or Moore, the man still had to get his son. Daughters are just place holders – practice critters, non-furry pets to give a woman diaper-changing experience until she can build that boy."

"You sound a little bitter," William said.

"No more than you," she shot back, her eyes narrowed in rage.

"I'm sorry. That's not what I was trying to say." William looked at her in a different light. "What I meant is that men and women don't get to be our age and remain single without a few – how do I say? – nasty ruts in the road, a few detours that sent us away from our original destination."

"Ruts, hell. Mine were sinkholes the size of a house. And the detours were through minefields, sending me to hell for… Well, for too long before I got here."

William grinned at seeing her nod of agreement. He held up his apple juice box in salute. "Here's to surviving the battle of the sexes."

Abe returned the toast. "Or of the exes. I guess it comes back to what we were talking about earlier. Idiocy, genius, orneriness: none of them have anything to do with age, gender, or ethnicity."

"May our days of dating frauds – our nerves frazzled from trying to keep sane – be in our past, our futures filled with…" William blinked, trying to finish the toast, his brain fog returning.

"May the rest of our lives be blessed with boredom and routine," Abe finished.

"Yes, yes. And may we always have someone nearby to finish our projects or sentences, whichever are needed."

"Or both," Abe said.

William downed his drink then set the box down on the table with a thunk. "Do you do that all the time?"

"What?"

"Always insist on having the last word."

"I didn't have the last word, William. We're still talking. I really think you ought to go to bed or at least kick back with a book or the newspaper. You're getting a little out of sorts."

"I am not."

Abe looked down her nose at him and nodded.

"I repeat, I am not."

She nodded again and whispered, "See, I didn't try to get the last word."

He whispered back. "And yet you did."

She shrugged. "Okay. I'll leave so you can 'not get your rest.'"

"You did it again!"

"Sorry."

"Forget it. Let's see what we have in the way of frozen food. Would you do the honors? It's a bit difficult for me to check."

Abe bent over and looked in the freezer. "Chocolate ice cream?" she asked without turning around.

His eyes widened at the view. Tight jeans across a round rear end. "Um. No. Keep looking."

"That's right. Chocolate is brown. Hmm. There are frozen hash browns…"

"Brown. At least, they will be if you cook them right."

"Brussel sprouts?"

"Not brown but they should be. Nope. Is there any frozen chicken in there? Even canned chicken will do."

Abe shuffled aside a few items, then stood up and shut the freezer. "Nope. Absolutely no canned or frozen chicken in there. However…"

She opened the cupboard door above her, then went to the next one until she'd opened them all. "Shoot! Where do they keep the canned food around here?"

Eyes wide at the sight of her bosom heaving from exertion and ire, now only partially contained by two buttons, William gulped. "Um, around here, we have a pantry for dry goods. We…we generally don't keep canned food in the kitchen."

Abe saw where he was looking and frowned. "Where?" she growled.

William's head snapped up. "Sorry. I've lived alone too long. I'm not used to women at all. I mean, you're a fine-looking female and decently put together, but honestly, it's just the novelty of having a real human being right here – so close and alive. It's your face, not the back of your head I'm seeing, a flesh and bone entity, not an image on the television or computer screen. Please forgive me."

"Well, when you put it that way, I know what you mean. Before I moved here, I was a bit of a loner myself." As casually as she could, she glanced down and fixed her blouse closures. "Would you believe that at my previous residence, I never once let anyone inside the front door?"

"Hmm. Come to think of it, other than Joe when he and the realtor showed me this place, you are the only person I've been in this house with. I mean, the cleaning lady comes and goes, but that's always when I'm not here."

The moment of awkward silence was broken when Abe asked, "Where's the pantry?"

"This way." William led the way, picking up and setting down his walker with stifled groans of discomfort.

"You could have just said, 'Over there,' you know."

"Well, you've heard about that damned English pride, I'm sure."

"No, not really. Actually, no, not at all. Now, male pride, that I'm familiar with. Go ahead and sit at the breakfast bar. Maybe your canned goods assortment is better than mine."

"Remind me to make sure The Home Team doesn't bring anymore canned chili," William called out over the clatter of her moving about cans and bottles.

"Amen to that! Hey, do you like tuna?"

"Fresh or canned. No, scratch that. Yes, I love fresh tuna, but we don't have any. I can tolerate the canned variety as long as it's albacore, not that brown meat garbage."

"You really don't like brown food, do you?" Abe asked, a can of albacore and jars of mayonnaise and pickles snuggled up to her chest.

William looked at what she had, then realized where he was

looking. "Sorry. I really was looking at what you brought out. What's your plan for a meal?"

Abe laughed. "Careful, William. You might ruin your reputation as an ornery old coot. What I'm making is a college student dinner. Sort of. I saw an assortment of chips behind the bar. With what I have here plus a little chopped onion and pepper, I can make some crackerjack finger food. Messy, crumbly, sticky-beyond-napkins, finger food. Do you trust me?"

"Hmph. Joe has trusted you with my life. I guess I can, too. May I help?"

Abe started pulling out drawers, then answered when she found what she was looking for. "Yes. Would you rather open jars or chop onions?"

He pointed to the appliance on the counter. "Electric bottle, can, and jar opener. I believe it would be easier for you to do that chore. Hand me a cleaver, cutting board, and bowl. Get ready to be amazed."

Abe put the jars and can on the counter and set up the chopping board while William washed his hands. "OCD?" she asked.

"Obsessive Compulsive Disorder?" he said as a question. "No. Occupational Cleanliness Demanded. My mother was a nurse. She insisted on handwashing before and after just about every task. She's eighty-eight and still hale and hearty. She must have done something right." He came back to the counter and patted the spot in front of him.

Abe set the knife, cutting board, and onion down. "Here you go."

William smacked the whole, unpeeled onion on one side, then turned it around, attacking all sides. "Now watch this." He sliced off both ends, then made a shallow slit from top to bottom. *"Voila!"* he exclaimed as he peeled the papery skin away in one wide piece. "Works for garlic, so I figured it would work for all alliums. It looks like I was right."

"I'm impressed. How do you do with chopping it, though?"

William stood up, putting all his weight on his uninjured leg. Very dramatically, he brought the knife down with a loud *thunk*, cutting the globe in half. Then, as if on double or triple speed, he whack-whacked away, dicing the whole onion in seconds.

"Okay. Now I'm very impressed. Let's see if I can do just as good at opening cans and bottles with one of these."

Abe picked up the electrical opener and looked underneath and behind it. A broad grin came across her face as she figured out the basic principle. "Okay, I think I got this."

Clunk! Whiz… Clunk! Whiz… Clunk! Whiz…

In seconds, she had them all opened. "Now for the culinary magic." She grabbed a big bowl, the pepper grinder, and a spatula then started dumping and stirring.

"This is something I learned a long time ago. It's the same in all aspects of life as in cooking. Presentation is everything."

She filled two crystal bowls with the tuna mix, then set them on the serving tray with the rest of the silverware. "Shall we dine in the parlor, milord?" she asked with a feigned British accent.

William gasped and his eyes widened. Then he realized it was just part of her role-playing. "We shall, madame. Would you care to lead the way?"

"Um, it's this way, right?" she asked as an aside.

"Yes, correct. It is to the left."

A yelp escaped from William when he stepped wrong, his curse quickly stifled.

Abe looked back at him, making sure he was all right.

Lips pressed together tightly, he nodded his head. "I'll be fine."

"I take it you didn't finish your bottle of medicine."

"What was your first clue," he snapped, then immediately apologized. "Sorry. That was uncalled for. Yes, I was distracted. Actually, that – distraction – works better than whisky or pain relievers. Of course, the other two are usually easier to obtain."

"Well, I'll see if I can scout out some white wine. That is what you're supposed to drink with fish, right?"

William chuckled. "Yes. See what I mean about distraction? For a flash there, I didn't hurt at all. Let me apologize profusely in advance, though, in case I get out of hand. I really don't like mean people. When that mean person is me, it's even worse."

Abe stepped away from the table and took a bottle of Gray Riesling from the wine cooler. "Will this work?"

He nodded and looked down at his plate of peppered beige mush, then back up at her.

"Hold on. It's not ready. Let me get the glasses and I'll pour out. If I do something wrong, please correct me. Gently. I'm not a classy lady. Where I'm from, there's just beer and soda pop wine. Hoity-toity wines with fancy lettering and gilt-edged labels are only in magazine ads."

She pulled out the cork with ease and started to pour.

"First, let the wine breathe?" Seeing her questioning look, he said, "Just trust me. Part is tradition, part is letting the vapors from being bottled up for ages dissipate."

"Okay. That makes sense. While it's doing its little detox regimen, I'll get the rest of the meal."

Abe grabbed a new bag of potato chips from the cabinet in the game room, then ducked in the kitchen and brought the three different types of crackers she'd seen. "Sorry, but I'm too much of a practical person to put all these out in separate dishes. Just grab a fistful of each and put them on your plate. It's weird, but even though it's the same goop, the tuna tastes different on a potato chip than it does on a saltine or peppered water cracker."

William looked at Abe without emotion, his bottom lip out, eyes blinking but without letting her know what he was thinking.

Not knowing whether he was pissed at the paltry meal or having a seizure, Abe snapped her fingers in front of his face. "Hey, wake up. Are you okay?"

A quick intake of breath and he was back to the world of the living. "Sorry about that. I was just wondering, how would these taste on tortilla chips?"

"I don't know. Do you want to try?"

"Does the queen rule Britannia?" he asked. "Of course, I do."

The two spent the next hour noshing on poor-man's fare served on silver and crystal, splitting the bottle of wine as they recounted stories

73

of the most unusual foods they'd ever eaten.

"You know, I'm glad I didn't finish that whisky," he said, his hand coming to rest on top of hers.

She looked at it, smiled, then pulled it away gently, using it to bring her glass to her lips for a sip of wine. "Why didn't you want the whisky?"

He gulped in embarrassment, but they both ignored his subconscious pass. "Whisky and wine don't go together well in the gut. I'd have a hellacious hangover in the morning. I have enough issues without that."

Abe reached out with her empty hand and put it over his. "You'll be fine. We'll get you fixed up."

William looked at her hand, then up at her, and grinned.

Abe looked down and saw she had made the same hand-over-hand gesture to him. She pulled back. "I'd better get this mess cleaned up and go to bed. I think I've had too much to drink." *Or not enough.*

William nodded and agreed. *Not too much. Not enough!*

* * *

"What are you doing, woman?" Abe huffed at herself as she walked across the broad driveway to the shop. "You have enough complications in your life."

Pbbt! Her inner self blew a raspberry, as loud in her head as if she was her own twin and standing a foot away. "You haven't had a complication in nearly ten years. Well, except for that one-year tryst with that two-faced thief. 'Oh, it'll be fun starting our own business. With your repair skills and my salesmanship, we'll have contracts all up and down the river.' Well, at least I know William isn't after my money. Not that I ever had enough to attract anyone but a slimy, backwater gambler. Salesman, my ass. Pretty-faced con artist is what he was. Damn his hide, wherever it is."

Leftover rage at the lover who had stolen her heart and savings account, then spurned her, boiled hot. Furiously, she yanked open the door to the shop but once inside, she smiled. Head to toe glee washed over her like warm sunlight after stepping out from a dank mountain cave. She had forgotten the one treasure Rufus hadn't taken from her.

Her 1976 Norton 850 Commando was confined in the crate, but still closer now than it had been in days. With the income from this job, she could get new tires. The bald treads on it now would slip and slide on just about any surface. Her urge to ride was extreme, but she'd wait. That time would come.

She reached in and ran her hand over the front fender. "Welcome to your new home, Snortin'."

As tired and confused as she had been moments earlier, a jolt of adrenaline came surging through her at the touch. "Yes, you're still mine. Let's get you out of that cage."

Prybar in hand, she began disassembling the side of the crate first, making it easier to take off the dozen straps the shippers had used to secure her baby.

And then she saw it.

The little furry mass was curled up under the engine cylinders, his black and white stripes as vibrant against the shredded pale excelsior as if he was painted on a blank canvas.

"Hey, little fella. Are you alive?" she asked.

The little head lifted at her voice, then plopped down in the nest.

"Okay, Pepé, let me fix you up. I'm sure I have an apple around here somewhere. I'll cut it up for you so it's easier to eat."

Abe rummaged through the standup desk and found it. "Oh, here it is. See, I'll get you up and running in no time…"

Abe bit her bottom lip as she cut thin slices from the apple and placed them on a discarded plastic lid. "Check these out, my little stowaway."

Crouching near the wee critter, she held out a matchstick-sized piece of apple without peel. Pepé's nose twitched and his mouth opened. He nibbled half of it, then put his head back down, exhausted. "Are you sure you don't want more?"

With her encouragement, he stuck his nose in the dish of food, rooted around, but didn't eat.

"Okay, I understand. That's enough for now. I'll come and check on you later. Don't go anywhere, okay?"

As if to answer her, he opened his eyes and looked at her, then put his head down again and sighed.

"Well, I'm glad you survived the thousand-mile trip. This is my new home. I think you'll like it around here. I know I sure do."

***

Too embarrassed to spy on Abe as she danced and sang while she worked, William went straight to bed. The half-bottle of whisky was sitting on the dresser, calling to him with its siren song of oblivion.

"Not tonight, drink. Three Ibuprofen should work well enough. I don't want to forget this evening. Besides, it's hard enough to keep my thoughts under control. That's all I need is to lose my grip on my words. I don't want to chase this one off. She's a real peach. Can't cook worth a damn, but she does know how to make a nice presentation. Oh, yeah…"

Chapter 7

Due to the absence of William Gagnant, AROUND THE WORLD IN 80 CARS has announced a delay in this year's episodes. The other two stars of the series – Morris Donaldson and Ben Zachary – are reportedly working on projects of their own. The show's producer, Joseph Patterson, denies the rumors and said they are still working together, patiently waiting for their beloved William to recover from his injuries. Still no word on his status or where he's recuperating.

***

Abe awoke with a hangover. No, hangover was only one word and not strong enough. A whole paragraph was needed to describe this agony. Needle-toothed maggots, nibbling the ends of her pain receptors, anacondas strangling her upper chest, tigers with razor-blade claws shredding her stomach while elephants jumped rope on her bowels... Yeah, that began to describe it.

Those symptoms didn't even include the bladder discomfort, but she could take care of that with a pit stop. She smacked her lips. Her mouth was not only dry but felt as if she'd eaten a pillow. She pulled said polyester-filled form off her face. "Hmph. Not cotton candy then..." As soon as she moved it and the light hit her eyes, she put it back again.

"Who says light doesn't hurt? What's coming in now has to be laser level, at least." She lay still and conked out again until bladder urgency awoke her.

"No, no, no. Don't pee the bed. You're a big girl. Crawl if you have to, even pee on the linoleum, but don't wet the bed or soil the carpet, woman."

Abe squinted against the brilliant morning sun and stumbled toward the bathroom. One hand covering her eyes, she felt along the wall with the other, finding her way with eyes closed. "Oh, I am so not drinking fancy wine again."

A shower long enough for the hot water to run out ended with her dashing to the linen closet, searching for a towel. "Why didn't you put out fresh ones after you tossed the others in the dirty clothes?" she scolded herself.

Chilled to the point that her fingers were stiff and trembled, she dressed as fast as she could. "Coffee. I need coffee."

In the kitchen, she realized the comforting aroma of Columbia's finest was missing. "Damn! I forgot to set it up last night. Yeah, you were out drinking. Dining and carousing with your boss." A slight smile started. "Not my boss but not a bad dude, either. Once he gets healed, he might be a good one to take for a mattress ride."

Her stomach clenched at the words. "What's got into you, woman? Wait. Ride? Oh, my God! Ride! To hell with fantasizing about sex with a man who's out of my league, my ride is here! My Snortin' Norton…" She paused, remembering the little black and white treasure she had found in the crate. "My Pepé, too."

The maternal urge to check on her little stowaway motivated her to rush downstairs to the shop and make sure he was still alive. "Not that there's anything I can do beyond offering food, shelter, and water."

The black and white critter was as still as death but not dead. All the cut-up apple bits she had set out for him were gone, his belly bulging. Yes, and that little tummy was also moving up and down as he breathed. "That's right. You're nocturnal, aren't you, little guy. All right. You go ahead and get some sleep. I'll cut down a box and make a little condo for you later. My man is going to get his own place."

At the thought of 'my man,' her thoughts returned to the other male in residence. "I'd better at least offer the old fart juice this morning." Her eyes brightened. "And coffee for both of us."

After cutting up a few more pieces of apple in case Pepé woke up and wanted a snack, Abe beat tracks to the house. She bit back the desire to call out, 'Good morning, sleepyhead,' just in case William was also nursing a hangover.

As she stepped softly through the front door, William called out, "Care for a cup of coffee?" while saluting her with his mug.

"Oh, I certainly would," she replied, reaching for it.

He pulled it away. "Yes, me too. This one's empty. Maybe your barista skills are better than mine. I just threw out the pot I tried to make." He stuck out his tongue in an uncharacteristically childish manner. "Tasted like skunk piss."

She giggled, thinking of setting a tiny urine collection cup in front of Pepé to get a sample. "Have you ever tasted skunk piss?"

"No, but I doubt it could taste worse than what came out of that machine this morning. Would you do both of us a favor and brew some of that ebony elixir of the gods?"

"Well, I may have marginal cooking skills, but I do fine on coffee. I might even tell you the secret."

"I don't need to know as long as you're around to make it for me." William blanched at his suggestion that she stay around for an indefinite amount of time. "I mean…"

"Hey, don't worry about it. I have a hangover, too. Anything *anyone* says before the first cup of coffee is totally off the record and cannot be held against him or her."

"When did you get so smart?"

"Not smart," Abe said. "Maybe clever, and definitely empathetic, but smart usually comes with a degree. I didn't even get past the first semester of college." She took William's mug from him. "Come on. Let's go into the kitchen. You can begin your morning exercises by walking."

Abe went in ahead of him to get the coffee started. The pot in the sink said a lot. It looked like a fifty-percent slurry of water and coffee grounds in the bottom of the carafe. She poured it down the garbage disposal and rinsed it out. By the time she'd finished, William was seated at the breakfast bar.

"First step is to use very cold water." She filled the pot to the mark, then poured it into the coffee maker.

"Next, you put one, and only one, coffee filter into the basket." She demonstrated with an exaggerated flourish.

"Then you put two level scoops of ground coffee into the filter. If it's too strong for you, I can adjust it the next *times* I make it," she said with a wink at the word 'times.'

"My secret, though, is to add an itsy-bitsy amount of salt to the grounds." Abe sprinkled salt in her hand, pinched some of it between her thumb and forefinger, and added it to the grounds, dumping the surplus in the sink.

"Then all you do is slide it in here, put the carafe under it, and push start."

"I really don't know why you're showing me," he said, grinning wide, "if you're always going to be around to make it for me."

Abe shrugged. "It's a character flaw. I'm a born teacher. At least, I like to share." As soon as the last words were out of her mouth, she blushed.

William's eyes widened and he immediately turned away. She hadn't been looking at him when she said, 'I like to share,' and it might not have been an intentional flirt. Whether it was or wasn't, he wouldn't let her know he was aware of the possible Freudian slip.

She likes me. I like her. Two consenting adults, alone in the same house…

Yeah, and one of you is half-crippled. Keep it platonic. If she's interested, that little blush will grow until she's one red hot, willing and ready, mama!

"I said, do you want sugar or creamer in your coffee?" Abe asked again.

William shook his head in reply then groaned. "Ow. I guess that's one time when I should have used my words."

Abe started to nod in agreement, and they both giggled. "I think we should both just say no to non-verbal communication today. Anyhow, coffee's just minutes away. I'll see if there's anything to nibble on. I'm not an expert on hangovers, but I heard a little something in the tummy helps."

"Actually, from my own experience, it's wise to partake of the hair of the dog that bit you, some high carb food, and make sure you hydrate."

"Speak English, please."

"I am," William said, eyebrows narrowed in mock anger. "But I'll translate into American for you. If we had any of that same wine left, we would drink some of that…"

Abe groaned but didn't say anything.

"Hydrate as in drink lots of water…"

"I got that one."

"And eat high carbohydrate foods to raise the blood sugar. I guess it would work if we added sugar to our coffees."

"Black or even sweetened coffee would burn a hole in my raw gut, I'm sure." Abe opened the breadbox on the counter, looking for food. *"Voila!* Pastries."

"Saved by the Danish!" William added then winced as his head protested the excitement with a sharp pang.

Abe brought her hand up to contain her laugh. "I'm not trying to make light of your pain because I hurt, too. I'd do it all over again, though. I had a blast last night. I thought only young people were allowed to be silly."

"What do you mean? We are young people. At least, compared to my parents we are. I know they still have fun."

"Well, as soon as breakfast is over, I have a project and you have therapy."

"Not another appointment," William protested.

"Not today." Abe walked over to the coffee pot that was now gurgling, making its final brewing noises. "Your torture appointments in town are only three times a week. However, your daily exercises are just that: daily."

"Yes, yes. Range of motion and moving this aluminum frame from here to there, three to four times a day for at least ten minutes at a time," he groused.

"Did they say whether or not you could work out on a treadmill? I know there's one here, but I haven't seen you on it." Abe set Danishes on two plates and handed one to him.

"That's because I can't stand that thing. Actually, I hid the magnet that turns the monster on. It won't work without it." William took a bite of the pastry then puckered in distaste. "I'll wait for the coffee."

"The weather is beautiful today. Is there any reason you can't walk outside?" She poured the coffees and joined him at the breakfast bar.

"Other than I'd be in trouble if I fell and couldn't get up again."

"Meh. You'd only be in trouble if it got cold or you were in the way of oncoming traffic. Not much chance of either."

William started to protest but she cut him off. "But since I'm going back to the shop anyhow, would you like to come see my baby?"

"You have a child?" he asked, then brought the cup toward his mouth and savored the aroma, hiding his shock at her comment.

Just as he was getting ready for his first sip, Abe said, "Snortin' Norton."

William sputtered, spraying coffee a foot in front of him. "What? What kind of name is that to give a child? And who said you could bring a young one here?"

"Hey, hey, hey," she scolded, wiping off her blouse and handing him a fistful of paper napkins. "My Snortin' Norton is a '76 Norton Commando 850 motorcycle. He may be old, but he's in great shape. As soon as I get a few bucks, I'll get new tires for him. Then he'll be as handsome as the day he hit the showroom floor."

"Wait. It's here? Your Norton motorcycle is here? In the shop?"

"That's what I said. Or meant to. I just came in to check on you and see if you had any coffee." Abe broke her pastry in half and dunked it in her cup. She tried a nibble, then dunked it a second time. "These are better when they're a few days old. They hold more coffee that way and break apart less." Just as she said it, a piece fell into her cup. "And that's why I have the spoon ready."

William copied her gesture and dunked his Danish. Even though it was drippy, he managed his first bite without making a mess. "You're right. Much better. I can feel the sugar going into my bloodstream." His second dip and nip wound up a dribbly mess on his chin.

"Messy but worth it, right?" Abe asked, making sure he wasn't embarrassed. She quickly dunked and without trying, made a mess even bigger than his.

"Before I finish, you might want to bring the paper towels. I'm afraid these flimsy napkins aren't up to the task."

Abe set the entire roll of towels on the counter. William tore off a six-foot length and made a comedic show of wiping his face from his eyebrows to the middle of his chest – his hands, from dabbing fingertips to scrubbing elbows. "Oh, here. Don't let me keep you from your ablutions."

Abe took the paper towel roll from him, tore off a few sheets, and did a quick overall swipe. "I'm a low-maintenance kind of gal," she said, chuckling as she wadded up all the used paper towels. "I'll clean up this mess unless you want another Danish."

"No, no thank you. I would be grateful if you poured some of this delicious coffee in a thermos for me, though. See, my walker even has a cupholder."

Abe cleared the counter – setting cups and saucers in the dishwasher – and poured the last of the coffee into two brushed aluminum thermoses.

Abe and William were ready for the day.

And finding out more about each other.

"Yes, I think I can make it to the shop," William said, breaking their comfortable silence. "If you'd spot me, though, I'd appreciate it. This walker may be labeled all-terrain, but I don't know if they tested it on gravel paths."

Leading the way, Abe opened and closed house and shop doors for William. He faltered on the uneven ground a few times, but she stopped herself before offering a hand. She'd seen it in his personality that first day. He had enough pride for two men. It didn't matter if she was a man or a woman offering help. He was determined to make it on his own. Assistance was for weaklings and that was *not* how he saw himself.

"So, that's your Snorting Norton?" he asked, his elbows shaking with fatigue as he made the last few steps toward the crate.

"*Snortin'* Norton," she corrected. "It has to rhyme."

Abe noticed his minor trembling but didn't want to call attention to it. "If you'd like a front row seat to the unveiling, I'd suggest you get comfortable." She dragged her shop stool next to him. "This might take a while. I want to reclaim the crate's lumber for another project. Otherwise, I'd rip right through it to get to my baby."

At the word baby, she froze.

"What's wrong?" he asked as he sat down on the integrated seat of his walker, ignoring the offered stool. "It looks like you've seen a ghost."

She shook her head then winced at the pain. "No, not a ghost." She sat on the stool next to him and grinned nervously. "But he does have white on him...not that ghosts are white except in comics," she added. "His is a long double white stripe down his back."

"I'm sorry. What are you talking about?"

Abe moved aside the board sheltering the dozing Pepé. "He stowed away. He's pretty tame. I used to leave food out for him at my old place near the swamp. As far as I know, he's never sprayed anyone. I thought he was dead when I found him last night, but he was just hungry and dehydrated. A lot of folks keep skunks as pets."

"I didn't know that. How strange. I'm not familiar with their odor, but I've heard it's horrid."

"Yes, it is. The only time I've smelled it, though, was when I drove past a dead skunk on the road. I can relocate this little guy if I have to, but I don't want to do that until I'm sure he's healthy."

As she began her narrative, Pepé lifted his head. He blinked sleepily as she spoke, and if it was possible for a skunk to do so, smiled before going back to sleep.

"I think he likes you," William said softly. "Do you think you can uncrate your motorcycle without disturbing him? I'd hate to get him upset and set off his... Well, you know, his defense system."

"Well, I was going to build a little house and litterbox for him. He seems happy for now, nestled in the packing material. To be on the safe side, I won't uncrate it now. How about we check out my other project? Do you know anything about cars?"

"Other than they crash and burn if you're not careful?" William joked, then groaned. "Yes, I know about them, but I'm not a mechanic if that's what you mean. Even if I were, I wouldn't be much help. As banged up as I am, I don't think I could torque a head bolt if my life depended on it."

"If you've got your wind back from our hike from the house, it's time for your second workout." Abe walked away from him so he couldn't see her smirk. "Come over here and see the project my niece's husband sent me."

The clank-clatter of moving the walker ahead of him spun her around. "Wait!"

William froze in place and looked up at her. "Yes?"

"Weren't you using a cane yesterday?"

"I was."

"Why aren't you using it now?"

"Have you ever tried to sit on a cane?" he asked with a broad grin.

"Nuh-uh."

"I anticipated mobility challenges today, after the workout they gave me yesterday. I was right, too. I hope to be back to cane-level walking by this afternoon, though."

"Here's hoping tomorrow's appointment doesn't set you back again. If it does, I'm going to give that tech a piece of my mind. Or the toe of my boot."

William's head snapped back. "Why?"

"What do you mean, why? Because, well, I don't want anyone to hurt you. Or hurt anyone for that matter."

"Aw, my young female protector," William teased.

"I'm not that young," Abe chuffed. She looked down at her chest. "But I am definitely female. And it's part of my job to protect you."

"I'll agree with the first two but not the last."

Abe looked down her nose at him, eyebrows narrowed, ready to protest.

"Now, don't get all pissy. Fixing coffee for me, finding hidden bottles of whisky, and driving me to my torture appointments are all part of what you were hired for. I assume. I doubt risking life or limb was in the contract."

"So, if Pepé does get all excited, I don't have to step between you and him and take a stink spraying for you?"

"Well, I didn't say that," William joked. "Now, what is the surprise in that container? Although, I think I have an idea what it is."

Abe lifted the tarp off the crate, exposing brand new fenders, door panels, and cartons of MOPAR auto parts. "Ta-da!"

"Have you seen what's in the other crate?" William asked, his bright mood suddenly somber.

"Just a little bit of it. Joe told me what it was. I didn't want to get too far into it before I had my other project done. That one's parked in the shed for now."

"What other project?" William asked innocently, his head turned away so she didn't see his rapid blinking of guilt. *She must never find out you were spying on her as she worked and danced!*

"Oh, there was an old John Deere four-wheeler the previous owner used for checking fence lines and hauling stuff. Cyrus – the guy who used to oversee this place when Joe was around – was thinking of converting it to electric but gave up. I, however, never give up."

William chuckled. "Is that why you're so hard on me?"

"Well, I'm sure you'd be hard on me if the tables were turned."

William blushed when she said, 'hard on me' and had to turn away again.

"Why do you keep looking away from me?" Abe asked. "Is there something on my face?" She picked up a clean shop towel and wiped her mouth and nose. "Did I get it?"

"No. I mean, no there's nothing on your face. I keep looking away because... Hey, wait a moment. You said your niece's husband hired you. Are you telling me that Joe Patterson is a relative?"

"Not really. We're not related by blood, but his wife and I are. It's one of those not-too-common circumstances where the aunt is younger than the niece. Only by a couple of years, but we have fun with it. Now, if you don't mind, I've been dying to tear into this crate to see the rest of this. An honest-to-goodness 1964 Mustang! Man, how I wanted one of these when I was growing up."

She pulled the tarp the rest of the way off. Stunned, William collapsed against the brace of the walker's seat. "No wonder everyone was so freaked out," he said softly.

"What are you talking about? And are you okay? You look like you've just seen a ghost."

"That's the car I was in when I had the accident. Do me a favor, go over to the driver's side door and open it."

"Or what's left of it. Oops. That was tacky. Sorry."

Abe tore off the yellow caution tape. She gave it and the note attached to it to him. She tugged, pounded, kicked, and did every trick she knew to open the caved-in door, but it wouldn't budge. "Maybe if I used a pry bar or fired up the torch and heated the metal, it would open. But I don't think anyone could open it like it is with just bare hands. Maybe the fire from the wreck twisted it out of alignment."

"They told me the door was incapable of opening, that I climbed through the broken windshield." William looked up at her, ashen. "I don't remember it at all, other than waving everyone away. I smelled gasoline. I thought it was going to blow up. And it did."

"But you're here now." She put her hand on the side of his face. "You're alive and will be back in tip-top shape in no time, I'm sure."

"Did you know I had three broken ribs? They're still tender. My collarbone was broken so badly, they had to put a metal rod in it. And my femur was completely dislocated at the hip. The doctor told me there was no way I could have walked on that leg. Hell, look at me now. It's been over two weeks and it's all I can do to cross the yard. Can you imagine me crawling out of that," William pointed to the compressed area where the windshield had been, a scant ten inches wide, "and walking twenty feet away afterward? On a leg that was out of joint?"

"Miracles do happen, you know. At least, I believe in them." Hoping to change the subject, she asked, "So, what's that in your hand. I didn't look at it."

"It's a note to you, actually. That is if your name is Agatha."

"Grrr. I bet it's from Joe."

William chuckled. "Yes, it's from Joe. So, Abe is just a nickname?"

She shrugged.

"Don't tell me it's short for Abraham."

She growled again.

"I've heard of many women's names that are traditionally masculine or that can go either way, but not Abe. If it's not short for Abraham, what is it?"

"It's my initials. If you were a woman, would you feel comfortable being called Agatha? Or Aggie? It's fine…if you're a mystery writer or a college football player."

"Cheer up. You could have been given a name shared by literally millions of people in your country. William, Bill, Willie…"

He stopped when she giggled. "Yes, being called after a great American president is much better than being called a Willie."

"Or Tallywhacker."

"Or Dick… No, please stop. You're making me laugh and that hurts."

"Oops. Sorry." She looked away, then back at him with a smirk. "Sort of."

He waved one hand in the air as if erasing the moment in time. "Seriously, we have to stop. What does the note say, if you don't mind me asking?"

"'If the old fart wants it back after you've fixed it up, tell him *tough*. I said no more fast old cars without rollbars, air bags, and fire-suppression systems. Enjoy the project. Here's hoping Forever, Montana is your new forever home.'"

"Old fart, am I?" William asked, stifling a grin. "Is that what he calls me behind my back or what you call me?"

"Well, you aren't exactly a young fart," Abe teased. "And before you get carried away on this line, remember; you asked me not to make you laugh."

"Touché. So, are you going to rebuild the car?"

"I'm definitely going to explore my options. On the plus side, I have just about everything I need. Or so Joe said. I also have a shop to rebuild it in and time to do it. With those three biggies on the plus side, it's going to take one mighty big negative to offset them."

"How about obsession?"

"What do you mean?"

"I mean," William shifted on the seat and leaned forward intently, "I wanted to race that car in the land it was born in. Getting that Mustang up to top RPM and on an American track was everything. There aren't many of that year left and most have the smaller engine. It was almost a fluke, finding it. I have to wonder if it was fate tempting me..."

"Pause right there, please. I believe in miracles, not fate. You were *heavily desirous*," she said, rolling her eyes at the words, "of racing that particular car. That may have clouded your judgment in speed or whatever caused the accident. I'm sure it wasn't your driving skills." She looked uncertain. "Or was it?"

"The *lust,*" William dragged the word out and rolled his eyes like she had, "of driving that car clouded my judgment of which track to use. Even monster trucks shouldn't have been allowed on that mess. The surface was crumbling away, potholes and cracks everywhere. Even when used as an open-air market in the Arizona desert, it was in such a state of disrepair that the owners shut it down for resurfacing. The paving project was delayed, but I didn't want to wait another month for it to be done. I talked the owners into renting it to me for a one-time event. I twisted the arm – figuratively – of the associate producer, and he said let's go for it."

"Wait. What? Associate producer? Was this for a movie or something?"

"Or something," William snarled, angry at himself for the slip-up. With great difficulty, he stood up and positioned himself behind the walker, scowling with self-loathing and ready to leave.

"Hey, don't get mad at me," Abe walked in front of him and looked him in the eye. "You don't have to tell me if you don't want to.

I doubt it's important. We've been getting along fine. Don't go getting all…all…stuffy on me."

"Stuffy?" He took a step back and looked her up and down. "What in the hell do you mean 'stuffy'?"

"Upper-class crap. I got enough of it when I lived in Saint Louis for a month. I was the hick from the sticks. No one called me that, but they didn't have to. As soon as they heard me ask a question or make a comment, their noses went up in the air and they turned away."

"But your accent is charming."

"It wasn't that as much as the clothes I wore, the way I carried myself, whatever. I didn't stick around to find out. My dreams of an engineering degree vanished. I went as deep into the bayou as I felt comfortable with and made my own way. I picked up piecework, repairing whatever was broken. Pretty soon I had a great reputation. If it had gears or a motor, I could fix it."

William turned around in place and sat down on the walker seat again. "Really? That's fascinating."

"You're not mocking me, are you? Because if you are…" Abe looked around at the huge shop, full of every tool and device a mechanic could want, then over at the stairs that led to her magnificent apartment. "Let's just say, I hope you aren't. I *really, really* like this place. I even like you… even though I didn't think I would. I'd give it all up, though, if staying here was at the cost of my integrity."

"I am so sorry, Abe. That was not my intention. I know about cars. Actually, I know quite a bit about them. But I can't do much more than drive them. Repairs are beyond me. I did know Cyrus – the maintenance man – but he was skilled, not clever. You did say you finished the ATV conversion, right?"

"Nice segue, Sir William," Abe said with a broad smile, his unintentional insult forgiven.

"Now, are you mocking me?" he asked, voice chilly.

"Gee. I guess I was. Damn. If we're going to get along, I think we both need to get thicker skin. Truce?"

William stuck out his hand. "Truce."

Abe shook it and suddenly felt naked before him. Vulnerable. She shook off the titillating feeling. She'd save it for later. Right now, she couldn't let him see his simple handshake had aroused feelings that only her toy boyfriend, Titan, had stirred lately.

William brought his hand back to the walker. Weird. When was the last time he had touched a woman for any reason? Suddenly, their silence was awkward. Without thinking, he uttered, "Uh-oh."

"What's wrong? Did I shake it too hard? Is it your shoulder again?"

"Neither. I got a tingle."

"You have to tinkle?" Abe stepped back. "Don't let me get in your way."

"Tinkle?" William paused to figure out the connotation of the Americana word. "No, I don't need to urinate, I...I..." He shook his head vigorously, trying to dislodge the unexpected emotion. "I'll let you get back to work."

"No, please don't leave. I'd like your input on the Mustang. I'll bet you know more about them than I do."

"Instead of starting on that, do you think you could you bring Zippy – or whatever you call it – around? Maybe we can take it for a spin."

"Zippy?" she asked, smiling at the clever title. "Yeah, I like that name. It's still early, but we can make the rounds. I don't know how others do it, but I figure if I offer the horses oats or alfalfa every time I go out – no matter what time of day – they'll get used to me and come closer."

"I don't want to tame them," William said, a hint of reprimand in his voice.

"And neither do I. However, when it's time for the vet to visit, you won't have to hire someone to herd them in. Not that I wouldn't like to see a real cowboy in action…"

"Just go get Zippy. We can talk about cowboys and rodeos on the way out."

Chapter 8

Attn: William Gagnant. The Full Order of Protection filed against Eddie Rizzo aka 'Razor' Rizzo will expire five days after the date of this notification which is when the period of his psychiatric evaluation has been completed. If you wish to renew the order, please make an appointment with the Clerk of the Superior Court for an appearance before the judge. Be prepared to provide evidence as to why the Full Order of Protection should be extended. (Legal correspondence lost among the five bags of get well letters sent to William and held at Joe Patterson's office.)

***

After Abe helped him out of the re-powered Zippy at the front door, William shuffled inside and collapsed on the first soft chair he could find, letting the walker fall to the ground with a clatter.

"Life is so much more work than physical therapy." He looked at the liquor cabinet and chuckled. "Every bone and muscle in my body hurts but for the first time I can remember, I don't want to numb it. Pain just means I'm alive." He sat forward and his back twinged. "Well, maybe a little less discomfort would be okay."

William took the phone out of his pocket and dialed. "Okay, Joe. Where'd you put the next bottle? And before you ask; yes, I did my exercises today. If I hadn't, I wouldn't be hurting so bad."

Joe huffed in reply. "If I ask Abe, would she tell me the same thing?"

"Yes, she would. She's putting Zippy away right now. After that, she's making a new home for Pepé. Since I'm supposed to be on R and R, that's what I'm going to do: rest and relax."

"That's rest and recuperation, William."

"Okay. I'll take that."

"And who in the hell are Zippy and Pepé? Are you two opening a bed and breakfast or something?"

"Zippy is what I call her electric all-terrain vehicle. Oh, and she got the crate with the remains of my death trap and your note. To correct your assertion, I am not an old fart."

"Okay. You're a young fart with a lot of miles, then. Oh, wait. Before we start arguing about how old or young of a fart you are, I have to tell you that the weirdo who said he was your psychic twin was released from the mental institution. They couldn't keep him any longer. Or he escaped, I'm not sure. Either way, he's on the lam."

"You mean that kid called Saber or something?"

"Razor. I don't know if he's harmless or not, but it's best to lay low for a bit longer."

"Hell, Joe, I wouldn't mind laying low for the rest of my life. You were right about this place. I like it. Shoot, I could even go so far as to say I love it. The distraction, the beauty, it even smells great around here."

"Are you talking about the ranch or Agatha?"

"Abe," William corrected. "She's right, Agatha doesn't fit her. Now, tell me more about what's going on with this Razor character. Is there a warrant out for his arrest? I'm pretty sure the restraining order on him is still valid."

"It probably is in New York, but you're in Montana."

"Does he know where I am?"

"William, as far as I know, no one knows where you are. There's a lot of speculation. Shoot, someone even started a crowdfunding account to reward whoever discovers where you are. It's more of a gambling pool. People around the world are throwing money at it. The first person to find you wins the whole pot, less admin fees, which I'm sure are exorbitant. Someone's making a fortune on the search whether you're found or not."

"Ugh. How in the hell can I stay out of sight with that going on? How much is it up to?"

"Enough to buy anyone's dream car or a middle-income house. William, I've changed my mind about your physical therapy appointments. I know the therapist won't come out there, but do you think Abe would be willing to help you out? If she drove into the clinic, they could show her what's needed. That way, she could work you over in the privacy of your own home. I'm afraid someone's going to recognize you."

"Too late for that. There were at least a dozen people at my appointment yesterday, waving and calling out." William chuckled. "Abe thinks I'm a famous author."

"Yes, she did mention something about that. I didn't correct her, and neither should you."

"Well, we almost butted heads a few minutes ago on that same subject. I mentioned the word associate producer. She thought I had something to do with making movies."

"What did you tell her?"

"We agreed not to talk about it. She really is a… Oh, hi, Abe."

Abe grimaced at her intrusion, catching him on the phone. "Sorry. I guess I should have knocked."

He shook his head minimally and pursed his lips. "Then I'd have to get up to answer the door. You're fine. I'm talking to Joe. He's going to tell me where the next bottle of whisky is. Would you confirm that I've been eating and getting plenty of exercise?"

Abe took the phone from him. "Hey, Joe. Yes, William has been a great guy, taking his walks without squawking or throwing hissy fits. We got off to a rocky start, but we're on smooth gravel now. Okay, I think I can find that one easy enough. I'll let you know if we need anything." She handed the phone back to William and walked away.

"Um, William, what's this if 'we' need anything?" Joe asked. "You're not putting the moves on my wife's aunt, are you?"

William glanced up. Abe was at the bookcase, reaching for the top shelf, checking titles as she pulled down one book at a time. With arms up and on tiptoes, her perky denim-covered bottom peeked out from her flannel overshirt. "Oh, I'm sorry, Joe. What were you saying?"

"You're watching Abe right now, aren't you?"

"Just making sure she knows where to find the whisky," William said coolly. "Don't worry about us. We're both adults. And since we haven't killed each other in the first twenty-four hours of living on the same property, I don't think we will."

Joe chuckled. "By the way, I'm sending you a list with some of the ideas the guys and I came up with. I won't tell you which were mine and which were Morris and Ben's, so you're not prejudiced in picking out your top seven favorites."

"Well, odds are I'll be able to tell just by looking at them. But Joe..."

Abe stepped off the dictionary she'd been using as a stepstool and turned around to smile at him.

"Yes..."

He began again, "Don't bet on me coming back to work. I might just take a medical retirement. I have to go. Bye."

Abe smiled at his remark, so unlike the man she'd met only yesterday. "You're too healthy to take a medical retirement. Or you will be."

"You and I know that, but I don't want Joe to know. I'll let him find a good replacement for me or reconfigure the show so no one will miss me."

"Show?" Abe asked, curious but not eager to pursue his slip and possibly upset him.

"That's what I call it. A dog and pony show without dogs or ponies. You know, the same old 'Get clients, make them happy, all while keeping the profits up, and holding onto your integrity.'"

"You call readers clients?"

"Whoever buys into your product or service are clients," he said with a non-committal shrug.

"I guess that's true. One of these days, I'd like to read one of your books. Are any of them in here?" she asked, shuffling through the titles again, checking for his name on the spines.

"No."

She turned to him. "Why? Do you write erotica and think I'm too young to read it?"

"No."

"Or that I'm too innocent?" She batted her eyelashes and smiled coquettishly, then chuckled.

"No. I wouldn't be so bold as to judge your level of life experience or...or..." He pursed his lips and huffed, "You're exasperating, woman."

"So, I've been told. Then, where are they?"

"In process. And I'm only writing poems these days. My journaling days are behind me."

As Abe walked away from the bookshelves, her eye caught the glimmer of a gold-colored frame off to the right of the hearth, on prominent display but safe from smoke drifting from the fireplace.

"What's this?" She stood in front of it, her head moving side to side, squinting as she tried to read the fading elaborate script, penned in various shades of black ink. It appeared to be an ancient document that had been added onto for generations, the later entries easier to read. The border of the tannish vellum – or maybe it was parchment – was decorated with Old English griffins and dragons, the capital letters of each additional entry ornate and colored in bright red, blue, or green. Although displayed in a place of reverence, she hadn't noticed the historical document earlier.

"Oh, nothing," William said, grabbing his walker and rushing as fast as his broken body could to stand between her and the gilt-framed patent family tree. He reached up with his good arm, trying to take the family's crest and lineage record off the wall, and stumbled backward into her.

Abe righted him, then patted his back and moved him away gently. She finished the frame removal task but not before she had read the name on the bottom line: Sir William Richard Aldridge, born the thirty-first day of October in the year of our Lord, 1964.

"Here, I've taken it down for you. Where should I stash it?" She hefted the three-foot-by-three-foot frame again with both hands. "And is this gilt with real gold?"

"Hence the use of the name gilt. Yes, it's real gold. Otherwise, it would be just a painted frame. Although since it's made from oak, it would still be heavy. The amount of gold used in its finish is minimal compared to the weight of the wood."

"A simple yes would have done," Abe said as she looked around the room. "I'll stash it in the corner while you make up your mind where you want it."

"Oh, just go ahead and hang back where it was."

"What? Then why were you in such a hurry to take it down? Was it because you didn't want me to see you're some sort of royalty? Your real last name is Aldridge, isn't it?"

William shrugged, acknowledging the name without saying so. "Gagnant is my...um...pen name.

"Gagnant?" Abe asked, a confused frown appeared, quickly replaced by a grin. "Gagnant. Oh, *Gah-nyone,*" she repeated, using the French pronunciation. "Got it."

William's head twisted like a curious owl as he looked at her.

Abe was sporting a freshly-polished smirk, pleased with herself about something she'd just figured out.

William huffed. Busted. "Yes, yes. Evidently, you speak a bit of French. I know it means winner when pronounced correctly. Few people have picked up on it. It's sort of an inside joke for this old racecar driver...enthusiast."

Abe chuckled. "Kind of hard not to pick up a little Creole while living in the bayou."

"I am not royalty," he insisted, chin out

Abe tipped back the document and looked at it again. "No, just a direct descendent of William the Conqueror."

William rolled his eyes. He couldn't help but smile in satisfaction. He quickly overcame that damnable family pride and scowled. "Well, everyone has to come from somewhere, don't they?"

"Yeah, I guess. This is quite a bit different than my heritage. *My* ancestor was one of the women of the Salem Witch trials. I mean, obviously not one who was burned at the stake but one of those acquitted. While your great-grandfather was claiming the throne of England, mine was being tried for witchcraft."

"Well, about six hundred years apart, but yes. Yet, here we are, both standing in front of the same fireplace in Forever, Montana."

"Yup, the Conqueror's kid, all bungled up from not being able to wrangle a skinny-tired, vintage '64 Mustang, the witch's little girl twisting nails out of crates, pulling wrenches, and feeding skunks."

"I take offense at that remark," William said, his reverie shattered.

"Which one or ones? You all bungled up or the description of how your lack of skill got you that way?"

"B…Both!" he stammered.

Abe looked down her nose at him and raised an eyebrow.

"As you would have seen if you looked closer, I had the widest tires possible put on that Mustang. Lack of skill wasn't the reason for the accident. A poor driving surface was."

"You know, it seems like we just had this conversation. How about we agree not to keep coming back to the same old stuff? There's nothing we can do to change the past. We can only repair the damages caused by it and work on our futures."

"As I asked before, Abe, how'd you get so smart?"

"Repeating the question? Isn't that having the same conversation?"

"It isn't. At least, not until you give me an answer. Evasive dialogues don't count."

"Okay. The answer is, I learn from my mistakes. Since you think I'm smart, that must be because I've made a lot of mistakes in my life."

William chuckled. "Well, if that's the case, I'm a genius."

***

"Hey, Ford, do you think she was lying to us yesterday?"

"Huh? Who?"

Razor snarled. "That hardcase bitch at that big ranch in Forever."

"Oh, yeah, her, the one you were flirting with. You know, she *was* kinda slick. I mean, hot in a way for an old broad. Goin' back over what she said, though, she never came right out and said he wasn't there." He nodded and pursed his lips. "Yeah, one hot mama."

"Get your mind off getting laid. I wasn't flirting. I was just trying to get information from her. You can do her if you want, but William's my spirit brother. I hurt right here," he rubbed his blubbery belly, "without my twin close to me."

Ford looked down at the fuel gauge and rolled his eyes. "Well, wherever we're going, we'd better stop for gas first. This Focus of yours gets great mileage but it still needs a fill-up every now and then."

Razor reached into his front pants pocket and pulled out his wad of cash. He counted it out. Only ones left. Bribing the therapist at the physical therapy clinic had cost him more than he'd admit to Ford. It was five hundred dollars, not fifty, he'd given him. Still, it looked like the guy had been telling the truth. He'd have to get creative on buying gas and food until that reward money came in. Maybe his twin would spot him a thousand or two…

He looked over at Ford, still as clueless as ever. "Stop at the first small station you find. I don't like going to those big truck stops. Too many people with germs. Find one of those Mom and Pop places. I'd rather give the business to the little guys. Plus their fast food is better." *And, they're easier to rob and less likely to have security systems linked to The Cloud. I learned a thing or two watching cop shows for ten years.*

***

"If you don't need me, I'm going to the shop and get started on Pepé's castle."

William looked up at Abe standing by the front door, his unopened bottle of whisky in hand. "Do what you have to do," he said coolly.

She smiled broadly, unintimidated by his pout. "You know, having a goal or a project makes life so much more enjoyable. Achieving it gives a person a great sense of satisfaction. Plus, the journey is enjoyable if you've picked the right objective. It also keeps you busy and doesn't give you time to mope. You ought to try it sometime."

"Having satisfaction or a project?"

Abe leaned forward and asked, "What do you think?" and winked. "Call me if you need me. You have my number."

William waved her away with the glass he held as she left. He hated to admit it, but he truly was sad to see her go. Now, to watch her leave, that was another matter. A slight grin grew. He'd have to thank Joe for giving him fantastic scenery for inside the house, too.

He set down his ice-filled tumbler and looked from it to the bottle. "A goal or project, she says. I hate to say she's right, but she is. Maybe I'll build a little castle of my own, a brickwork of poems to support my lie about being a poet or author or…" William stood up straighter at the thought of creating something rather than wallowing in self-pity. He inhaled deeply and gasped.

Back spasm.

"What did the therapist tell you yesterday, Willie? Stretch those muscles before working them. And hydrate!" He put the whisky in the bar refrigerator and swapped it for a bottle of spring water.

"I never thought I'd chose drink that came straight from the ground over distilled spirits." He shook his head and fumbled for the pen and pad on top of the bar. "Or write poetry."

He twisted off the bottle cap and sat on the barstool. "Think, man, think." He poured the water, swirled it and the ice cubes in the tumbler, and stared at the blank paper.

"Okay. Now I get it. Writer's block. Just write something, even if it's crap." His mind came back to the Mustang Abe would be working on soon. Did he want to help her with it?

'Round and round the racetrack it goes,
The Mustang chased the record
To see how high the tachometer rose,
Pop! Goes the engine!

"Except it wasn't the engine that blew. I guess that's poetic license. How about another topic?" William looked around the room and noticed the interlocking double rings holding the draperies back. "Aha!"

The bridal reception
Turned to lies and deception
Flirting and groping

Turned to humping and hoping
Until all in attendance…

"Damn! This really isn't as easy as I thought it'd be. How – and why – do poets put themselves through this?"

William set down the pen and looked at the books on the shelf. "This would be much easier with a thesaurus." He scanned the titles and pulled a first edition of Julia Child's Mastering the Art of French Cooking from the bottom shelf. Joe's wife had given it to him years ago. "Hmm. Dorothy is Abe's niece. Who would have thought they were related?"

He lay the book on the bar and went back to looking for literary reference materials but came up empty. "I guess the dictionary will have to do." Still on the floor from where Abe had left it as an impromptu stepstool, William bent over to pick it up. He yelped, stopped by a twinge in his lower back.

"I'll let her deal with it when she comes back. Enough of trying to be a bard. That's not the road I want to go down." He picked up the cookbook. "Until I figure out which one, how about we go in the kitchen, Julia, and see what raw materials we have?"

Time flew as William flipped through the cookbook. He tore off strips of paper from the notepad he'd written his odes to race cars and wedding attendees, using them as bookmarks for the simpler recipes.

"I can do these. As long as there is butter, cream, eggs, and a bit of flour in the house, I should be able to prepare any French dish." He read past the ingredients on the recipe he'd chosen and grunted. "I have the components but not the equipment. What in the hell is a springform pan?"

Changing his tack to finding recipes that required pots and pans he knew were in his kitchen, William looked at the ingredients next. Narrowing his list of projects down to three, he decided on a simple soufflé and set to work. "Dinner and dessert in one dish."

***

Abe set up her music, choosing her custom playlist of Michael

102

Jackson tunes. Prybar in hand, she began tearing apart the crate that held the Mustang. Her fingers itched to start on the one containing her motorcycle – and her little stowaway – but she was pretty sure her actions would disturb the varmint. Whether he'd sprayed her in the past or not, she didn't want to startle him here, especially inside a building.

Unable to stay away from the weak but intriguing little creature, she set down her crowbar and knelt at the skunk's side. "Good morning, sleepyhead. Do you like 80's pop music?"

At her voice, Pepé looked up at her, one eye open. He swiped the air with an outstretched paw, then brought it back to rest on his chest.

"Would you like me to scratch your chin?" She reached toward him, letting the scent of her hands linger near his face. "Are you like a dog? Do you need to know what I smell like first?"

In answer, he reached out again. "All right. Here goes, fella. You be good to me, and I'll be good to you." When she scratched the little hairs on his bony chin, he clutched her finger with both paws and hugged it.

"You're just like a kitten. Oh, I so want to keep you as a pet. From what I hear, winters are tough around here. I'll give you a nice warm place to sleep if you let me pet you every once in a while. We all need each other, little guy, and don't let anyone tell you otherwise. Touching another being – whether human or a four-legged critter – is underrated."

Brrng! Brrng!

The proximity alarm rang, startling both Abe and Pepé. Fully awake, the little skunk ran for the shelter of the excelsior packing material but didn't give the little 'thump-thump' tail-up warning of impending spray that skunks were known to do.

"I gotcha, buddy. Let me take care of this one. If I need help, I'll ask."

Chapter 9

News item: A new version of the 'Angel or Alien?' video depicting the rescue of racecar driver and reality TV star William Gagnant has gone viral on YouTube, breaking previous records for views. Earlier editions of the video were blurry, with bright spots obscuring the person or creature supposedly assisting Gagnant from the burning car. This new, high-definition copy should put to rest all previous speculations.

In local news, authorities were dispatched to Elks Horn, Montana this afternoon when a silent alarm was triggered during a robbery. After filling his car with high-octane gasoline, a young man entered the store with an empty laundry basket which he filled with fast food, energy drinks, and candy bars. The thief held convenience store owner Omar O'Hara at bay with a long-handled razor and forced him to empty the cash register before duct-taping him to a support beam. Very little cash was taken, the owner said, as most of his business is transacted with debit or credit cards. Authorities say to be on the lookout for a blue, late-nineties sport edition Ford Focus with custom wheels. Another person may or may not have been in the vehicle. Suspect may be dangerous. Do not approach and notify authorities if seen.

***

Razor walked briskly back to the car, resisting the urge to run. "Get out, Ford. I'm driving. And put this in the back seat. I got us some snacks for the road."

The young man saw the fire in his road trip buddy's face and complied immediately. He'd known from the first hour of their 'Find William Gagnant' journey that Razor was a little off – and his temperament mercurial, especially if he got hungry. This was a side he'd never seen, though. "Anything you say."

As soon as the food basket was in the back, Razor popped the clutch and the Focus surged forward.

"Damn, dude," Ford screamed, scrambling to get in. "Can't you even wait 'til I'm in?"

Razor stomped on the brakes, allowing his weak but necessary partner to climb in. He sped away and noticed Ford buckling up. "Seatbelts are for pussies."

"Yeah, well, I'd rather be a live pussy than a dead duck. Damn, what happened back there?"

"Do you really want to know?" Razor asked, fixing the terrified man with an evil glare.

"Um. No. Just watch the road, will ya?"

Razor swerved and got back on the pavement, a plume of dust marking his erratic trail down the shoulder behind him. "Gotta get this steering linkage fixed one of these days," he said, chuckling at his lame excuse.

Ford gulped but remained mute. He'd learned long ago that it was best not to argue with a drunk or a crazy person. Razor was stone-cold sober but as nutty as a case of Georgia pecan rolls. He'd have to wait until the next pit stop to get away from him, though. Here's hoping the man would make at least one more stop before crashing.

***

William set aside his walker and used the marble countertop to help him get around the sunny room. He hummed upbeat random tunes as he scouted out where whisks, spoons, and bowls were stashed in the huge kitchen.

An hour and a half later, the simple soufflé he'd created was out of the oven. The lopsided main dish took longer to put together than he'd thought. He checked the clock again. "Lunch, not brunch then. It looks so naked, though. Hmm."

He set paper lace on the pedestal-style platter he'd found, then carefully transferred the soufflé onto it. A small corner of the eggy cake broke off in the process. He pushed it back into place, turning the imperfect side to the back. "Just like life, hide your flaws rather than stress about them. Now, what would Abe do to make this more appealing?"

Back to the refrigerator, he found fresh strawberries and

blueberries. He rinsed them in the colander and set them aside but kept searching. "Colorful but not quite enough."

A big grin arose as he remembered a trick he'd seen somewhere. He scooped a couple of tablespoons of powdered sugar into a small strainer. Holding it over his flour and egg creation, he tapped the side, dusting the soufflé with fine, white sweetness.

"As beautiful as the first snow of winter covering an amber field of wheat. Hmm. Maybe I could write poems about food."

William checked the clock again. With all the time he'd spent on his project, he hadn't once thought about his pain or wanted whisky. The two Ibuprofen he had taken when he first began may have had something to do with that, but Abe was right. Having a project to work on – a goal – really did make a difference.

Plus, he and she could enjoy the result of this venture together. Another meal to share.

He grinned. How many times today had the thought of her caused him to smile? Shoot! She didn't even have to say a word or even be in the same room to give him the warm fuzzies. "Hmph. There's something I really like about that woman. Whether it leads to something serious or she's only a crush, I'm glad she's in my life. Gawd. How did I get so sappy?"

William washed his hands again, humming, "Oh, what a beautiful morning," as he went back to his creation. Alternating strawberries with little triplet clusters of blueberries at the base of the soufflé, he soon had a colorful carousel of food.

He took a picture of it with his smartphone. "Hmm. Another angle just to make sure I have landscape and portrait versions. Who knows? This might be the start of something big. Instead of a show about fast cars, maybe I'll do one about fancy food made simple. I can have that show shot right here, too."

He looked at his creation again, peering at it from directly overhead, and saw what was missing – an accent piece. He placed an ornate, sterling silver serving spatula on the plate, and took another picture. "Gorgeous. Now, once I'm dining with that lovely lady by my side, my project will be complete."

Phone still in hand, he chuckled. "Speaking of lovely lady, what's that little minx up to in the shop? Has she started working on the Mustang yet?"

William sat down at the breakfast bar and opened the security app. He grimaced as he quickly scanned all the video views first, saving the shop images for last. "Who could possibly find me here in Forever, Montana? Stop being so paranoid, Willie. I'm sure no one followed us home from the clinic. You're imagining things. Besides, what is there here to steal?"

He chuckled as he realized what he'd just said. "You said, 'Followed us home,' old man. Joe was right. You truly are smitten, aren't you?"

***

Rather than blast her usual dynamic rock and pop tunes, Abe scrolled through the menu and settled on musical soundtracks from the fifties and sixties. "They don't write songs like Rogers and Hammerstein anymore, do they?"

Leaning over the stand-up desk, she made a rough sketch of Pepé's cardboard condo on the old calendar desk pad. She added dimensions, then stood back and looked over her design again, verifying her numbers. "One piece of triple-ply cardboard from that crate of replacement parts ought to do it."

T-square and marker in hand, she bent to her task, drawing the pieces of her pattern on the crate's lid. She considered using the electric jigsaw to cut them out, then decided against it. "Don't want to awaken my striped Prince Charming, do I? He needs his recovery sleep."

Time flew as she aligned straight edge and box knife, using the razor to cut out pieces faster than the power tool could have. With masking tape holding the aligned pieces together while the glue set, she was done in less than an hour.

"Your castle should be move-in ready by the time you wake up this evening, little guy. Rather than paint it, though, I think I'll shingle it with twigs and leaves. That ought to make you feel more at home."

Abe sat back down and twiddled her thumbs for a moment. Curly was singing a love song to Laurie. She sighed, a big smile growing as she identified with the couple who didn't quite seem to belong together but did.

"Oh, don't even go there, woman. He's a purebred and you're a mutt. Shoot, he's practically royalty. Hmph. Or he is royalty, but a thousand years removed from the throne of England. Still, even if you technically don't work for him, he is your client. Do not get romantically involved with that man. One wrong word and you're out of his favor. You'd be working under strained silence or worse, on the road, looking for another job. Who's going to hire a middle-aged female mechanic? No one. Listen to your own advice. Find a project and get on with it. The distraction of hard work will make you forget more than just physical pain. Remember, love hurts."

Abe checked on Pepé again. He was still asleep, his tummy moving up and down in a slow and steady rhythm. She blew in his face. He twitched then smiled but didn't awaken.

"Time for some work music, then."

The volume not as loud as she'd set it for her evening work sessions, Lady Gaga came blasting through the speakers, the momentum of Poker Face invigorating Abe as always. Hips and shoulders wriggling in time to the music, she danced over to her next project: the Mustang.

Alternating between hammer and prybar, she soon had the crate completely disassembled. She took several breaks in the process to check on the skunk, making sure the clunk-creak-clatter of boards being broken apart and tossed aside hadn't upset him. "That's my boy. Get used to me and the sounds of mechanickin'. This baby-blue pony needs a lot of work done to it. And I'm just the gal to do it."

***

"Damn! Why can't I hear what she's saying?"

William realized what he had just said and closed out the app. He set the phone on the counter, disgusted with himself.

"Stop spying on her. How would you feel if you found out she was stalking your every movement, recording every word, tracking *you* like you are her? Hmph. So, I've become the very paparazzi I detest? Get a life, Willie. If you like her, court her. Or at least upgrade that client and assistant relationship into a close friendship."

He looked at his culinary creation. "Take a walk to the shop. Impress her with the fact that you're exercising without being harassed to do it. Invite her to have lunch with you, maybe open another bottle of wine…" He shook his head. "Scratch the wine. Sparkling cider won't give us hangovers."

He chuckled. "There you go again, referring to the two of you as us. Better snap to it now, though. A soufflé is best eaten fresh."

Invigorated by a new goal, William was out the door and on the path in record time. He was proud that he had made the trek unassisted. No doorman required. And he wasn't as tired as he had been the first time.

William stopped to compose himself and catch his breath before going in. Abe was listening to pop tunes, the steady beat so catchy, he caught himself nodding in time to the music.

Suddenly, the door pushed open, nearly knocking him off his feet.

Abe lurched forward and caught him about the middle, bringing him upright, making sure he had his balance before letting go. "Oops! Sorry. I didn't know you were here."

William pursed his lips, biting back all the snappy answers that came to mind. *It's my home, so why wouldn't I be here? Do I need to make an appointment to come into my own garage? If I'd knocked, would you have heard me over that racket you're playing?*

Instead, he swished his glower into a grin, recalling her quick reaction and the spontaneous hug they'd shared. "Thanks for saving me," he said, adding a sincere nod of appreciation. "I just came out to get some exercise. And ask if you'd like to dine with me. I…I made lunch for us."

His cheeks burned, a slight blush rising at the word 'us.'

"It's real food, too," he added quickly. "A bit more than coffee and pastries. Not that those were bad…"

"Well, I don't know what you made, but I'm sure it's better than the tuna dip I threw together yesterday. I'm usually more of a fruit and veggies kind of gal, only using canned goods and chips to supplement those two food groups. Are you sure you'll be okay? We can ride in Zippy, if you'd like."

"Why don't we do that. I don't want to overdo the activity and suffer tomorrow. Plus, after dinner settles, I'd like to come back and see how your latest project is coming along. Who knows, I might decide to help with that old man-eater Mustang. Maybe you can give me a few pointers."

"It's never too late to learn. Plus, with this old car, it's pretty straightforward. Oh, for the days of carburetors, clutches, and fuses."

"Yes, yes. Before we were blindsided with oxygen sensors, electronics, and computers."

"I agree," Abe said. "If a car can run without them, why muck it up?"

Chapter 10

The latest version of the 'Angel or Alien?' video has been proved a fake! After intense scrutiny, the fan favorite and most watched video of the year showing William Gagnant being rescued from his burning vintage Mustang by a supernatural being has been proved to be heavily edited and amended with computer graphic images. The CGI enhanced edition is still gaining viewers over the original version submitted by ultra-fan Eddie 'Razor' Rizzo. Rizzo was unable to be reached for comment. His parents said he had left to find his 'spirit family' and good riddance to the troublemaker.

***

Ford was too tense to fall asleep. Razor had been driving four hours straight with only one quick stop at a gas station for fuel. Even then, he wouldn't let him out to use the restroom. Razor didn't come out and say it, but Ford figured Razor was afraid he'd split, maybe even call the cops on him.

And he was right.

On both counts.

It didn't take a Sherlock to figure out Razor had robbed that little convenience store gas station. The two of them were down to counting ones and loose change to buy food and fuel. It was his turn to pay, but Razor never asked for money, either before or after he went in. He also wore his broad-brimmed cowboy hat – which hid his face – and had put on his driving gloves before he went in. When he came out, he tossed them in the trash. The bushel of food he brought out to the car would have cost hundreds of dollars on top of the price of the high-test gasoline fill up. Unless Razor had some hidden cash or paid with jewelry, he'd robbed the store. By his cocky smirk and haste to leave, it was the latter.

Yes, it was best to play dumb with Razor.

113

It was also a good idea to part company with him as soon as possible.

And safe to do so.

Razor's head nodded as he drove, fatigue overtaking the adrenaline of the hunt for his idol.

"Are you sure you don't want me to drive?" Ford asked, intentionally startling him awake. "I know the way. You want to get there fresh, don't you?"

"Yeah, I do. And I will. Pop the top on another one of those energy drinks for me, will ya?"

Ford took the empty can out of the cupholder and tossed it on the back floorboard along with the others. "You only have diet ones left. Do you want one of them?"

"Hell, no. I got those for you," he lied. "Get me one of those Gold Lightning sodas. They have just as much caffeine and taste pretty good."

Ford twisted the cap off one and handed it to him.

Razor's hand shot out, reaching beyond the bottle, spilling it, nearly knocking it out of Ford's grip.

"Whoa, dude. I think you really ought to take a break. Your depth perception is screwed up or something."

"No. It's not!" Razor hissed, stomping on the gas to punctuate his declaration. "You moved it. Now, hold it still this time." He reached out and grabbed the bottle angrily, spilling the drink all over him, Ford, and the dashboard.

"You're gonna clean that up when we get to my brother's place," he snarled.

"No problem," Ford said meekly. "No problem."

Razor slugged down half of the bottle at once, then missed the cupholder when he tried to put it down.

"The bottle's too big for it," he grumbled. "Here. You hold it for now."

Ford reached for it, but Razor grabbed it back, spilling it again. "Never mind. I'll finish it. How far do we have to go now?"

"According to the map and the last milepost I saw, it's only eighty miles. That's just over an hour from here."

"At what speed?"

"That's at sixty miles per hour. That's what I've been driving. I don't know how fast you're going because I can't see the speedometer from here."

Razor stomped on the accelerator and surged ahead. The engine whined and tachometer pegged as it hit top speed. "One fifteen now, up from eighty. So, when will we get there now?"

Ford took out his phone and opened the calculator app. He tapped out the numbers then looked up and said, "About seven-tenths of an hour."

"Who in the hell tells time that way? What's that in minutes?"

Ford made another calculation. "Forty-two minutes. If you keep up this rate – and don't get pulled over for speeding – we should get there at noon-thirty."

"Hmph. Just in time for a late lunch." Razor rubbed his ample belly. "I am getting a bit hungry. I'd better eat something before we get there just in case he already had lunch. Hand me one of those sandwiches."

Ford unbuckled and leaned into the back seat. He rummaged through the empty wrappers and remaining food in the laundry basket. "All we have left are sandwich wraps. Do you want ham and cheese or a bean burrito?"

"I'll take the ham. I don't want to get there all full of farts. You can have that one."

"Thanks just the same, but I'm not hungry." Ford removed the plastic from the tortilla-wrapped sandwich and put it in Razor's hand, making sure the crazed man had a grip on it before letting go.

"Something wrong with you?" Razor asked. "You haven't said five words in the last four hours."

Ford settled back in his seat and buckled up again, pulling the seatbelt extra snug about his hips. He looked out the window as the terrain zipped past him at double speed. "Just saving my words," he said and continued with his non-stop silent prayers.

***

"You made that? All by yourself?" Abe asked.

William's chest puffed out in pride at the sideways compliment. "Do you see anyone else around here?"

"No, but. Dang! That soufflé is gorgeous. I can't wait to taste it. I wasn't that hungry until I saw it. Let me wash up and set the table. That's the least I can do since you cooked."

Abe went to the sink. It was piled high with dirty dishes. She grinned but resisted the urge to chuckle or ask how many bowls did he need to whip up one soufflé? She set the dishes to one side and washed her hands. "I'll take care of these later. I don't know how they do it in England but here in America, if you cook, the other person has to clean up."

"I never cooked before, so I wouldn't know. Would you like something special to drink or is sparkling cider okay with you?"

Abe dried her hands, tossing the towel on the counter. "Cider's fine. I'll grab some of those fancy glasses. Simple fare, elegantly served…"

"With good company, is a banquet," William finished.

"You're right. You are a poet, even if that didn't rhyme."

"I'm a work in progress."

"You mean, your poetry is a work in progress?" she asked.

"No. *I* am a work in progress. Come, let's eat in the dining room. Believe it or not, I've never taken a meal in there."

"Cool! We can initiate it, then."

Abe set the table with linen napkins, sterling silverware, Haviland china, and Waterford crystal. "I don't know much about fancy plates and glasses, but I do know what these are." She held up a champagne glass. "Do you think they're appropriate for sparkling cider?"

"Ah, when in Montana, you can do whatever you'd like. Within reason, of course. Simple cider. No hangover, even if served in a champagne flute, guaranteed."

The two sat across from each other at the table. "Shall I serve?" Abe asked, "or do you want the honors since you prepared it?"

"I think you're steadier on your feet and have better leverage. Proceed, if you don't mind."

Abe cut into the golden crust dusted with powdered sugar and the whole works caved in. "Oh, my. Is it supposed to do that?"

"I'm not sure." William took out his smartphone and did a quick search on the internet. "It says here a soufflé falls somewhat after the egg whites have cooled. The hot air in the whipped eggs cools and the whole works deflate. It's best eaten warm, right from the oven."

"But it's okay to eat the way it is now, right?" Abe asked.

William scrolled down the page. "Ah, yes. It doesn't harm the product, but the texture won't be as light."

"Okie doke." Abe set a piece on both plates. "Be right back."

William scowled, frustrated that his first try – which he thought a success – was also a partial failure. He looked up. "What do you have there?"

"Assorted jam packs and cream. You did say something about 'when in Montana,' didn't you?" she chuckled.

"Adaptation. The secret to survival."

Abe used her spoon to pluck a dollop of orange marmalade onto her slice of soufflé, then splashed a bit of cream on the side. "Let's see if this tastes as good as it looks." She bit into it. "Oh, yeah…"

William chose red raspberry jam and poured a heftier portion of cream onto his. He carefully cut off a small portion, inspecting it before bringing it to his mouth to make sure it had both jam and cream on it. He bit into it and his eyes widened.

"Oh. You're right. This is dessert and dinner in one. However, the next time I make this, I'll make sure you're home when it's ready. I want to see how it tastes fresh out of the oven."

"Home?" she asked softly.

William felt another blush rise. "Well, yes. It is your home for now. Or at least, the apartment is." *Separate residences…for now.*

Abe bowed her head, preparing another bite, making sure he

couldn't see her face was getting just as red as his. *He likes me! He really likes me!*

"Ahem."

Abe looked up. Apparently, William had either asked a question or made a comment that needed a reply. "I'm sorry. I was wrapped up in trying to figure out what jam I wanted for the next bite. Hmm. Or should I try it naked. I mean, bare."

William raised his eyebrows in mock shock, then laughed. "How did we ever survive eating meals by ourselves? I'm serious, other than when I'm working with a crew on location, I always eat alone." He shook his head and huffed. "I thought I was multitasking, reading contracts or work-related articles rather than pleasuring myself with... I mean, reading for pleasure."

Abe quickly put her hand in front of her mouth and swallowed hard. She took a sip of cider, then when she was completely composed, spoke up. "I take it 'pleasuring myself' has the same connotation across the pond as it does here? At least, by your grade-A bluster, it must mean something intense."

William winked and leaned towards her. "How about if we drop this line of conversation right away? That is, unless you want to see who can make who get the reddest."

"How about them Mets..." Abe said, lifting her glass in a toast.

"Excuse me?"

Now it was her turn to lean forward and speak softly. "It's a segue, an awkward but traditional transition to another topic of conversation in this country."

Abe waited for his response then huffed in exasperation when he remained dumbfounded. Silent.

"Mets. They're a baseball team... Oh, never mind. Hey, on a legitimate topic, are you sure you want to come over and help me on the Mustang? I mean, would it be too weird for you?"

"If it does get weird, at least I'll have you nearby to make me laugh." As soon as the words were out of his mouth, William put down his fork. "That was awkward."

"Only if we let it be. Come on. Finish your drink and I'll clear the dishes. If I don't get to them tonight, then The Home Team can take care of them tomorrow. Man, I love having someone to clean and shop for me."

"And cook for you," William added. "I mean." He held the glass in the air and inspected it. "Do you think that all fluids turn alcoholic when poured into a champagne flute?"

"Nope. But I don't doubt two adults who have been socially repressed for years can't help but entertain themselves with the silliest topics."

"Well, Abe. Do you think this will stop or slow down? I have a lot of years of repression socked away."

"Lord, I hope not."

"Come on. Leave the dishes. *We* have a project to approach."

While Abe cleared the table, William swapped out his walker for the cane he'd been gifted years ago when he'd sprained an ankle. "Never thought I'd need you again," he said.

"Need me for what?" Abe asked.

William squeaked in shock and stumbled forward.

Abe reached out and caught him. "Are you all right? I guess I need to make more noise or not come up on your blind side."

Still in her rescue embrace, William grinned. "If this is what it takes to be held by a beautiful woman..." he crooned, then winked and patted her on the shoulder, letting her know it was okay to let him go.

Abe sputtered and stepped back. "I'd say you did that on purpose, but I don't think anyone could fake a squeal that high."

William tried, and a croaking sound came out. "Yes, that's true. Come on. You can drive. That is your job, correct?"

A guttural groan escaped, and a frown washed over Abe, erasing the levity of the brief encounter, replacing it with embarrassment. She turned away from him with a huff. "Yes, sir."

"Whoa, whoa, whoa! That was a joke. Or meant to be." William followed her, stomping his cane into the earth with a quickened pace, trying to catch up to her angry exit. "Hold on a moment," he panted, stopping to catch his breath. "If I keep this up, I'll be on the ground. Then what will you do?"

She turned and looked at him. Desperation covered him from his sucked-in bottom lip to his hands clutching the cane's handle, his shoulders wavering as he tried to keep his balance. "I guess I'll just have to catch you again," she said, walking up to face him.

"Look, whether it was because of an accident or not, I liked it when you held me. I must admit, I'd rather be the one who makes the moves on a lady. However, at my age and state of health, I'll take what I can get."

Abe stepped back and glared at him.

"What?" William realized his mistake in word choice. "No, no. Not *you* are what I'll settle for. I'd choose you over any woman I've ever met." He paused, scowling as he thought. "Or even that I might meet in the future. Good grief, woman. As I said in the past, you're exasperating."

"I don't do it on purpose, you know."

"I understand that. But believe me when I say, you have skills, tact, an interesting point of view on the world, a brilliant smile..." He looked her up and down. "And are spectacularly well put together."

"Three days in each other's company and we haven't clobbered each other?" Abe asked. "Yeah, I'd say we have a good start on a healthy relationship. At least, for two seasoned, 'set in their ways' car enthusiasts. Come on. Let's go check out that Mustang. Like dining, maybe this will be more fun when done together."

Side by side, the two approached Zippy. "You can drive, if you'd rather."

William shook his head. "No, no. I'm still a bit gun-shy when it comes to taking the wheel. Why don't you take the long way around, so I can get in more sightseeing?" He looked her up and down with a mischievous grin. "And I'm not talking about the property, either."

"I can see why you drive fast cars. Once you get started, you really put the hammer down."

William shrugged his injured shoulder and gave an exaggerated

120

yelp of pain. "Maybe I start that way but once I find my path, I'd rather take it slow and steady. You know, enjoy every moment."

"Or moments..." Abe corrected. She held onto his cane as he climbed into the four-wheeler. "Come on. I owe you a ride. Oh, and that was a very nice meal, by the way. Thank you."

"Here's hoping we are able to share many more."

"Amen to that," Abe said, getting in beside him.

William huffed. "You're doing it again."

"What?"

"Having the last word."

Abe clamped her jaws, shook her head, and looked at him, lips tight in a thin line to keep from saying anything.

William sighed in exaggerated relief. "Ah..."

"See, I can be quiet," she whispered.

"Grr!"

They both laughed, then she turned to him. "Sorry. You're right. It's a character flaw. I'll try to fix it."

"Oh, please don't." William reached over and touched her cheek. "You're perfect just the way you are."

"Back at 'ya. Oops! I did it again, didn't I? Had the last word."

"You're perfect either way."

Abe took a detour to the stock tank. The couple enjoyed the near silence of their electric-powered ride, the soft whir of the wheels being driven reminding them how loud it would have been with a gasoline motor.

William rested his hand on her knee. "The quiet of this moment is even more special because it wouldn't be this way if not for you and your clever engineering."

"If we're saying thanks, then thanks for keeping me around after finding out I wasn't a guy. That was Joe's idea, not mine. Actually, he told me he intentionally left out any mention of gender when he suggested me for the job."

"Hmm. I don't always agree with him on everything, but I have to admit, his choices are generally spot on. I suppose that's why he's the produce…" William feigned a cough, then looked up at her.

"What? What's that *look* about?"

"Oh, hell, Abe. I can't lie to you, and I can't lead you on. Joe's my producer."

"Speak backwater hick American to me, William, because the way you say it, producer is something fancy like a man who's in charge of movies. If that's what Joe's job is, I'm pretty sure I'd know about it."

"Actually, you're close. He produces a television show, not movies." He shrugged.

"Oh." Abe paused and thought about what he had said, glad that he wasn't interrupting her thought process. "So, when you were talking about the associate producer the other day, were you talking about yourself or someone you work with?"

"Yes on the latter."

"Does that mean you're not an associate producer…"

William nodded.

"But you work with Joe and he's the producer."

He nodded again.

"Okay. Now I'm confused. Joe said he worked with you. I don't know a director from a producer from a gaffer. How do you and Joe work together and does it make a hill of beans difference when it comes to me? Or rather, to me and you?"

"That's a lot of questions…'

"I'll wait. I don't have a cake in the oven."

"First, I do give my opinions and input to Joe but not in those positions you mentioned. He's the executive producer of Around the World in Eighty Cars." William paused to see if she recognized the name. When she didn't flinch, he continued.

"As far as 'does it make a difference to you, or to you and me,' I don't know. I'm one of the three men on screen. We have quite a few fans. Generally, they're civil. However, the photographers who intrude on my life can get rather obnoxious. Since you are here – in my life with me – if they ever found out where I live, they could become a bother."

Abe listened closely to everything he said, not saying a word. William waited for it to sink in.

Suddenly, she sat up straight. "Oh, so you're not an author, are you? Those people who were waving at you at the clinic were people who recognized you from that time when you were on TV."

"Um, yes and no. Around the World in Eighty Cars is a television series that's been on for years. Actually, it is quite popular."

"Is it shown in the United States, too, or only England?"

"It's worldwide, hence the title of the show. Its popularity soars in the country we're filming in and pretty much continues after we've left."

"So, you've been all around the world?"

William nodded.

"Wow. That's cool. Oh, and in eighty cars: does that mean you get to drive that many different cars?"

"I've driven literally *hundreds* of models when you consider the different years, engines, configurations..." He looked at her and saw she not only understood but was radiant.

"Wow. That would be so cool. I don't know which one I'm more envious of – the number of cars driven or the travel to different countries. Shoot, I haven't even crossed into Canada or Mexico. I guess going to a border town in Texas one spring break in high school is as close as I ever got."

"Well, I'm not sure if I'm going back. It's rather intense. Gratifying in the ways you mentioned, but there are upsides and down to not sleeping in your own bed at night, eating your own cooking. Or someone else's who you know by name." He winked and smiled at her.

She grinned at him, then got that little mischievous twinkle in her eye again. "Do whatever you want about retiring or going back to work, but if I get a chance, I'd love to sneak up to British Columbia for a little peek see. You know, just to say I've been out of the country at least once."

"Let me get healed up completely so I can negotiate the terminals and airports. I'd like to see the world as an unknown tourist for a change. If everything works out, I'll take you wherever you want to go."

Abe pursed her lips and nodded, deep in thought. *If everything worked out between the two of them or he healed?*

William put his arm around Abe's shoulder and hugged her close. "What I meant to say is if I don't screw up and alienate you, I should be hale and able to cross wide terminals without a wheelchair in two to three months. Do you think we can stand each other until then?"

Abe giggled like a teenager at the attention and his words. "Will you keep cooking for me?"

"That I'll do. I think I've found a couple of new passions in the last twenty-four hours."

Abe tittered again and looked up at him, seeing the sprinkles of gold in his gray eyes for the first time. "Me, too."

"So, before I get too mushy then frustrated with this weakened body, would you care to take us back to the shop? I feel like I can handle seeing anything now. I have my protector at my side. That's twice, no, three times today alone you've saved me from a fall."

"Well, you were sort of trying to show off..."

"And you were almost a bit too eager to hold me..." he teased.

"I don't know about that, but I wasn't going to let you hurt yourself, whether I was working for you, or it was something else."

"I'm not sure what 'something else' you mean, but I hope it was that I am not just a fiscal obligation."

Abe smacked him playfully on the back, then put the ATV in drive and headed to the shop. "You're more than a client to me. Actually, that relationship shifted into friend mode when you didn't make a big deal about me having to take a quick detour and squat in front of the car to go pee. I was ready to hear at least six different smart-aleck remarks, but you didn't make even one."

"Do you want to hear them now? I did think of quite a few."

"Nope."

William looked back towards the house. A plume of dust was rising from a vehicle coming up the dirt road toward it. "I wonder who that could be."

Abe slowed down and looked. "Oh, shit!"

"Excuse me?"

"Sorry," she said. "You had a couple of visitors yesterday. Two men were looking for you. I knew they were fans but back then, I thought you were an author. Anyhow, I didn't commit to whether you did or didn't live here. I sent them on their way, telling them they were uninvited to this property."

"So that means they're trespassing, and I can call the cops on them. Hold still for a moment. I don't know if I can dial when you're driving over bumps."

William's call went through. "Yes, I'd like to report trespassers... No, they didn't commit any other crimes. At least yet... No, I don't know their names. There are only two that I know of... What do you mean? No, I don't want to talk to them. They were told to leave yesterday and now they're back. Isn't trespassing enough? It isn't? So, if they murder me or my gal, then you'll come out? Fine lot of good it does to have a police department... Okay, sheriff's department. Hello? Hello?"

William turned to Abe. "She hung up on me! That dispatcher hung up on me! Evidently, trespassing isn't a big enough crime to come out for. Now, if they do something major like murder someone, then they'll come out and add trespassing to the charges. Bah!"

"Well, let's hope these guys are just after an autograph, not your life."

"We might as well confront them on our own terms." William put his hand on her leg again. "Let's hope words are enough. I'm afraid that even on a good day, I'm not a good fighter."

Abe put her hand on top of his. "The right words will be enough, I'm sure. That and an autograph."

"Let me meet them as a man, face-to-face and standing upright," William said, struggling to get out and manage the cane at the same time.

Abe took his walking stick from him, letting him stand unaided. "I got your back, even if you hadn't just called me your gal." She came around beside him, cane in her hand in case he needed it, proud and straight in solidarity.

He held onto her elbow. "If you'll have me…"

"I'm your gal, then. Agatha Beatrix Evans. I guess since I know your real name, it's only fair that I should share mine, too."

***

Razor bounced up and down in the driver's seat as they approached the turnoff to the long driveway, too amped up on caffeine and adrenaline to sit still. "We're finally here, Ford! Finally here!"

"Yeah, and surprisingly in one piece and without a speeding ticket."

"That's him!" Razor squealed, pointing to the front of the big house in the distance. "I know it's him." He rubbed his eyes, making sure he wasn't hallucinating again. He turned to Ford. "That is him, isn't it?"

"Yeah, that's him. And her. I'd recognize her anywhere." Ford hung his head in shame, embarrassed to be returning under these circumstances.

Unable to contain his excitement, Razor stomped on the gas. Ford snapped back to attention and bellowed, "Hey! Slow down, dude! Remember, the traction on those cobblestones suck."

Razor dropped the car into second gear and took his foot off the gas, squinting at his idol still a hundred yards away. "Is he holding her hand, Ford?"

"Um, no. He's holding her elbow."

"He's touching her? He has a girlfriend? He can't have a girlfriend! No!" He gunned the engine and sped toward the woman at his spirit brother's side.

Ford saw what he was up to and grabbed the top of the steering wheel, pulling it towards him. The Focus swerved to the right, avoiding the handsome woman and man at her side, crashing into the decorative-stone front wall instead.

126

Ker-thunk!!

Pop! Pop!

Both airbags deployed and quickly deflated, saving the driver and passenger from a flight through the windshield or worse.

Abe thrust the cane into William's hand and rushed over to the bashed-in vehicle, pungent steam spewing from the radiator, the hiss the only sound from the eerily silent motor. The two men who had been there the previous day were both alive but dazed. Moans of pain and distress came from Abe's interceding savior while vehement curse words spewed from the would-be assassin behind the wheel.

"Stupid mother..." Razor looked up and saw his idol had arrived. "Oh, hi, William. I was calling out Ford, not you...brother."

William's eyes widened and forehead wrinkled, visceral rage working hard to wipe out years of diplomacy and reason. "Were you trying to run over my gal?" he asked through clenched teeth as the big man wrangled himself from behind the steering wheel.

"Who, me?" Razor wiped the sweat from his forehead with one hand, his upper lip with the other. "No, no. That's not what happened." He looked side to side, avoiding William's piercing glare, trying to find a patsy.

"Ford!" he pointed to the injured man Abe was helping out of the car. "Yeah. Yeah. It was him. I had a hell of a time trying to keep him from killing her."

"Me?" screeched Ford. "It was you, you...asshole! You're a freakin' lunatic. I thought we were on a road trip to find William, wish him a personal get well, collect the finder's fee reward, and maybe get an autograph. You're absolutely a stalker, man. And a thief and...and. Damn, dude! Did you rob that convenience store or what?"

Razor chuckled nervously, then saw he was cornered. Chest puffed with pride, he stuck out his bottom lip. "Yeah, I did. What of it? I needed fuel for both me and my car. Those stores have insurance, and I didn't hurt nobody." He whipped out his long-handled razor and twirled it around menacingly, then stuck it back in his hip pocket, adding a visual exclamation point to his excuse.

Huffs and tsks were the only reactions to Razor's feeble justification for the robbery. He looked to William – whose head was shaking in disgust – and his nervous chuckle returned. This wasn't how he expected the first meeting with his spirit brother to go. He pointed to the purloined bashed-in Focus. "Well, it looked a lot better two days ago. Maybe you and me can fix it up. Brother."

"What's this *brother* nonsense?" William asked. "And I'm not a mechanic. Even if I was, I wouldn't work beside you. You stole money to get here?"

"But I had to! And you have to help me fix my car, especially since that alien rescued you. Even beings from way out there," he clumsily grabbed his razor from his back pocket and used it as a pointer to indicate the broad expanse of blue Montana sky, "know how special you are."

"Young man," William said, taking a cautious step towards Razor, "What's your name?"

"Eddie Rizzo, sir. I guess you forgot my earth name. We've been spirit brothers since the start of time. You came to earth first, though, to pave the way. We're going to do great things." Razor stood up straight, shoulders back, like a soldier at attention, then stumbled. "I'm here now, ready to help you. Brother."

"When was the last time you slept, son?" William asked, quickly looking over to Ford for verification.

Razor rubbed his forehead, confused. Ford spoke up. "Two days, at least. I've been with him for that long and haven't seen him take a break."

"How…how can you stay awake that long?" Abe asked.

Razor glared at her interruption. "Who are you and why are you here? You don't belong here. This is a men-only site. We're all about fast tracks and fast cars, not fast women."

William took a step back and put his arm around Abe's shoulder. Out of years of habit from being a woman working with men, she started to shrug it off, then changed the movement and cuddled closer to him.

"She's my gal and belongs here," William said. "You, however, do not. Now answer her question."

"Huh?" Razor shook his head, fatigue-induced hallucinations of ravens and sparrows flitting about William's head confusing him.

"He's drunk at least a case of energy drinks in the last two days," Ford said. "I don't know how many he downed before he picked me up. I'm a fan of your show, but, man, I am not obsessed. Oh, nice to meet you, by the way. I wish it could be under better circumstances. Sorry about the mess." He nodded to the three-foot-high wall made from native stone. "I figured if I yanked the steering wheel away from him and he hit that, it would be a whole lot easier to fix than your lady friend." Ford waved meekly at her and smiled. "Hi."

Abe returned the gesture and gave a weak, "Hi," in return.

Razor stepped between Ford and William. "Enough about her and...and..." He looked at the ground, rubbing his forehead again, trying to sort his thoughts and erase the visions of earthworms and garter snakes writhing at his feet. As plain as day, he could see them but knew they weren't real. "What were we talking about? Oh, yeah. Cars. Is it here? Is your Mustang here?"

Abe nudged William and he nodded. He was thinking the same thing. If he distracted the lunatic, she could call for help.

"As a matter of fact, it is here."

"It's in that shop over there, isn't it?" Razor gushed, bouncing on his toes with uninhibited excitement. "I knew it, I knew it. See, Ford! I told you he and I were psychic brothers. That's where I would have put it, too."

"Yeah, well it is a garage," Ford said softly.

"What did you say?" Razor growled, his blade held up menacingly.

"I'll bet it's a nice garage," the frightened man said louder, changing his reply and hopefully fooling Razor.

Abe patted William on the arm and walked toward Ford. "Come with me into the house. I'll clean up that cut forehead for you."

"You're staying with us," Razor shouted. "Both of you. I don't trust either one of you not to call the cops."

"We better do what he says," Ford whispered to Abe, wincing in fear. "He's a loose cannon, if you know what I mean."

Abe frowned in uncertainty. "No, not really but yeah, I get the idea. William?" she looked up at him with eyebrows raised, asking wordlessly for direction. *Do you have a Plan B?*

William nodded in reply. "Let's go in the shop and look at the man-eating Mustang, shall we?"

Rather than agitate the delusional man further, William let Abe bring up the rear with the scared but brave young man wearing the Ford ballcap. He led the way, doing his best to ignore the muscle fatigue, concentrating on each step with the cane. *I have so overdone it today. I'll be feeling it in every muscle in my body tomorrow. If I live that long.*

As soon as he walked through the door, William hit the buttons on for all overhead doors, opening all four of them at once.

Razor spun around, confused by the roar of the motors. "Why'd you do that?"

"If you want to see the Mustang, I thought you'd appreciate brighter light. Would you like me to take a picture of you in front of it?" William asked.

His eyes widened, and a smile overtook his frown of paranoia. "You'd do that? Duh! Of course, you would. You haven't seen me in hundreds of years. Yeah, yeah. Go ahead and take a picture with my phone. Hey, Ford. You take it so my brother and me can both be in it."

Abe elbowed Ford, handing him her phone on the sly.

"Let me wipe my hands first," Ford said to Razor, stuffing Abe's phone in his pocket with the gesture to pull out a crumpled-up paper towel.

Razor took out his phone. The screensaver popped to life – the photo of him standing next to a cardboard cutout of William at a fan event.

"Hey, look, William." He rushed to his side. "That's you and me. Well, a *picture* of you with me – the real me. You weren't at that conference. I almost got a picture of me with Morris, but they ran out of tickets before I got there. The same thing happened when I stood in line for Ben Z. I kind of got asked to leave, but I'd already had this picture taken. Now I'm with the real you."

While Razor was babbling, Abe stood in front of Ford. Hands on her hips, she rocked back and forth on her heels, positioned as a screen for Ford as he furiously texted for help. Razor looked away from William at one point, scowling at her, certain she was up to something. "Would you like me to take a picture with your phone, William?" she asked.

He shook his head. "I didn't bring it with me," he lied. "One picture should be enough."

Brng! Brng!

William's eyes widened at the sound of his phone ringing in his pocket. "Well, I'll be."

He hastily read the text. 'RU OK?'

"I guess I didn't leave it inside, then. I'll just turn it off, so we won't be distracted."

Instead of turning it off, he hit dial and speaker, calling the sender. Joe.

***

"Oh, crap. Our worst fears have been realized."

"What's wrong, Joe?" Dorothy asked. "Did they cancel our flight?"

"No. Worse." Joe picked up his landline phone and dialed. "Remember that crazy man in New York who was stalking William?"

Dorothy nodded.

"Sorry, honey. I was talking to security. No, you're not honey, Sarge. Oh, so you do remember that nut, Razor. Well, he's found William at his place in Montana. Contact the local cops or sheriffs or whatever it is they have out there. I just got a text from Abe's phone saying 'Razor holding us. Danger. Come quick.' When I texted William's phone, asking if he was okay, he dialed me. I have him on my cell right now. I can't hear a damned thing, though. He must have

131

stuck it in his pocket. All right. Keep me updated. And don't call my cell. I don't want to end his call. Maybe he'll put it somewhere I can hear what's going on. Bye."

"So, Abe texted you?" Dorothy asked.

Joe shrugged. "Either Abe or someone who has her phone. I hope we're not being set up."

"You and me both."

Chapter 11

Update: Convenience store robber identified from surveillance video. Eddie 'Razor' Rizzo, has been tentatively identified as the thief and man who assaulted the store owner. Rizzo was formerly under psychiatric evaluation after he was caught trying to sneak into the hotel room of William Gagnant, one of the stars of the popular television series Around the World in Eighty Cars. The suspect is still at large and considered dangerous.

In other news: Edsel Wadsworth Worthington aka Ford is still missing after ten days. His mother is offering a $100,000 reward for him. 'Alive only,' she says. 'What good is a dead heir?'

***

Abe walked toward the open shop door, testing the peripheral vision of their captor.

"Get away from there!" Razor snapped. "You're not going anywhere until I decide what to do with you."

"Do with her?" William asked, shifting the side of his body with the cell phone towards Razor so Joe might hear him better.

"She's new, right?" Razor asked, rubbing his inner elbows against his body, itching all over but not wanting to scratch. "I've never heard of her, so she must have come into your life after the accident. She's a nurse, right? I'm right, huh?"

William ignored the first question but answered the last one. "No. She isn't now and never has been my nurse. The most I've ever seen her do in that regard is wiping the blood from your friend's forehead." He looked over at Abe. "The young man didn't need stitches, did he?"

"No. Just a shallow cut," she said, her fingers twitching away as if she were texting.

William saw the gesture then looked back at Razor to make sure he hadn't. The young man's eyes were fixed on him, blinking rapidly to stay awake, a slack-jawed smile of adoration on his face.

"You do know, you're responsible for this young man's injury," William said.

"I don't want to talk about his scraped forehead. He could have done worse than that skateboarding. I don't want to talk about girls or Ford or nothin' right now except you and what happened out in Mesa. Were they angels or aliens? You were the only one there close enough to see."

"Well, I'll tell you..." William said slowly, ignoring the shakiness of his steps, trying to get closer to both Abe and Ford. Two more steps and he was holding onto the wooden crate with the remains of the Mustang. He repeated, "Well, I'll tell you..."

Razor took the bait and leaned over the fender, getting as close as the burnt and twisted metal hull would let him. "Yeah...yeah? Which one?"

"I don't remember a blessed thing other than smelling petrol and telling everyone to get away."

"But what about the angels?" Razor shouted, not even trying to appear rational now. "Or were they aliens? You were there. You have to know!"

"I haven't even seen the video. Rather, videos. I heard eight more popped up. Did you happen to see them? I'll bet you have fantastic sleuth skills. After all, you did find me here."

"He bribed your nurse at the physical therapy clinic fifty bucks to tell him where you lived," Ford said. "Sorry, but I heard through the grapevine where you'd be. Otherwise, we never would have found you."

"Fifty bucks?" William and Abe asked at the same time.

"I'm only worth fifty bucks?" William whispered softly, humiliated.

"Five hundred," Razor admitted. "But I would have paid ten times that much...if I had it. Oh, and I will have it soon. There's a bounty on finding you. Ford and I were gonna split it, but I just got a better idea."

"Yeah," Ford said. "You can have all the money, get your picture taken with your idol, then leave us the hell alone. Go back to where..."

Thunk!

His fist wrapped around his razor handle so tight, his knuckles were white, Razor threw a right cross to Ford's chin, knocking him off his feet.

Abe saw it coming and caught Ford before he hit the concrete floor, his head cradled in her bosom. "Oh, thanks," he moaned, looking up at her with a confused smile.

"Yeah, sure," she said and helped him stand.

"There you go, Ford," Razor laughed. "You can have the girl and I'll take the money. Then me and my brother can travel around the world, racing the fastest, hottest cars ever made, without *her* hangin' around. After we're done with that, we'll come back here and fix cars."

Halfway through Razor's rant, William realized he wasn't being watched. He pulled the cell phone out of his pocket and – hidden in his palm – slid it onto the desk, speaker side up.

Razor spun around and caught him as he pulled his hand away. "What in the hell is this?" He picked it up and looked it over. "This ain't mine."

Eyes red-rimmed with rage and two and a half days of no sleep, he brought the handle of his blade down repeatedly, smashing the phone, sputtering as he ranted. "Try and pull one over on Razor Rizzo, will ya? Don't push me too far or I just might give that little old mama to Ford as damaged goods."

William stepped back, more shaken than he ever thought possible. This man was crazy and volatile. What could he do to get out of this?

"Hey, buddy," Abe called out. "What did you say your name was?"

"Eddie Rizzo,' he snarled, "but you can call me gone."

"Okay, Gone. You said you were the one who robbed that store, right? You must be pretty slick to get away with that? How'd you do it?" *That's right. Start blabbering, get him to talk about himself, eat up time until the authorities get here. Maybe cool him down, too.*

"First thing you do is not get seen." Razor anxiously rubbed his chin with one hand, then the other, then with the first one again. He walked towards her, intent on telling her – or anyone who'd listen – his success story. "Wear a disguise and gloves or at least a hat that hides your face and hair."

Razor's antsy scratches and twitches continued as he rambled on, disclosing details of the heist until he saw Abe glance sideways at one of the crates on the shop floor. "What's in that?" he growled, paranoid that she had a plan to take him down.

"Didn't you want to know how we did it?" she asked, noticing her backpack next to the wooden crate that held her motorcycle, hoping she hadn't focused on it or that he'd seen her interest in it.

"How you did what?"

"The aliens. They have to live somewhere, don't they?" she asked, batting her eyelashes and smiling, gritting her teeth in self-control. *Walk with him, woman. Make sure you're close enough to knock him senseless with your bag.*

Abe approached the crate from the other side, getting near him but not close enough that he could grab her. She led him around the partially exposed motorcycle. Hopefully, Pepé would be startled by him and do his thing. It would be worth getting exposed to a stink spray if she and Ford could disarm and subdue Razor afterward.

Arm out straight, Razor pointed his blade at her. "Stand back, woman. I don't trust you." He squatted beside the crate and looked inside. "What's this? I didn't know they made red, white, and blue Goldwings?"

"It's not a Honda, moron," Ford said, cradling his battered jaw. "Even I know that."

Enraged, Razor shoved the top of the wooden box, trying to push it over. It scooted a few inches but was too bottom heavy to be knocked over. "Well, I know one thing, it's not a Harley, so not worth shit."

Ignoring his rants, Abe circled around, looking for her skunk. The little nest he'd made in the excelsior was empty. She looked at William, eyes wide, and shrugged.

"Rizzo," William called out.

Razor spun around, his snarl now a smile. "Yes?"

"It's a Norton. They're made in my home country. Country of origin isn't an indicator of worth. It's the engineering and materials that go into a product that determine its value."

"Yeah, yeah. You're right. Brother," Razor said, giddy again, his moment of rage evaporating as he neared his idol. "There's so much you can teach me. I...I'm ready to learn."

William forced himself to focus on Razor, keeping the mercurial man's attention as Abe figured something out. He'd have to trust her. There was nothing he could do.

Whoot! Whoot!

Razor spun around at the sound of sirens approaching.

Thunk!

Razor's head snapped forward and he faltered a step but remained upright with the blow.

Abe had swung her backpack as hard as she could – and made full contact – but hadn't brought him down. Now she was trying to regain *her* balance, her arm numb from the strike.

Not to be outdone, the enraged Ford raced toward Razor, ready to tackle him and knock him the rest of the way off his feet. "Argh!"

Razor saw him coming and stepped sideways, avoiding the tackle. He knew his time was up or getting there. Two sheriff's vehicles were close. He couldn't stick around. From the doorway, Razor spotted the primer-gray ATV, his getaway vehicle. "They'll never take me alive!" he crowed dramatically as he raced toward Zippy, the four-wheeler.

Ford started to pursue him, but William put his arm out. "Hold on," he said. "That ride is so slow, even I could catch up to it on foot...with or without this cane."

Ford's eyes were sparkling with admiration. William had his hand on his shoulder, holding him back, carrying on a personal conversation, saving him from possibly more harm. "Thanks, sir."

Abe rushed over to William's other side. "Pepé's missing. I looked again. He's not in the crate."

"Who's Pepé?" Ford asked, his eyes on the sheriffs' cars pulling up towards them.

William was still focused on Razor. Unable to figure out the ignition of what he must have thought was a gas engine, he was no longer confused but was stomping on the floorboard excitedly, screaming at high C pitch. "Look, Abe! I think he may have found your little friend."

Two sheriff deputies raced toward the idle four-wheeler and would-be thief, then suddenly pulled up short. "Oh, my gawd!"

"What's the matter…" Ford asked, then pinched his nose. "Don't tell me. Pepé's a skunk, right?"

Abe pushed the garage door buttons and gently pulled the two men inside. "Let's keep the stink out there. I'm sure Pepé will be fine."

"Just to be sure," William said. He stepped outside the man door. "Leave the skunk alone," he hollered to the authorities. "He's a pet and just protecting his owners."

"Or domain," Abe added. "I think the sheriffs aren't too keen on bringing him in. I'll bet they're wishing they could haul Razor back to town in a trailer, though."

"Or strapped to the roof," Ford said, and the three chuckled.

"So," William said, addressing Ford as the officers dealt with the stink and stinker outside, "did you come out here to meet me or get the reward?"

"Actually, sir, it was to meet you. I kind of wanted to find out about that miracle or those aliens or whatever saved you. Since I'm here, do you think I could take a look at the Mustang?"

"Come on over. You've earned at least that much."

William led the young man to the crate, the cane tapping the way across the concrete floor. "See," he said, pointing with the carved willow walking stick. "That's where I came through." He patted his slim belly. "I'm not so skinny that I shouldn't have made it, but you see how I'm walking now. I was even worse then. No, I haven't seen any of those videos, and I don't remember much, but I have a bit of muscle memory of feeling hands under here, lifting me." William set the cane down and indicated his armpits.

"So, you think it was angels or aliens?" Ford asked.

"I'd say angels. I've seen enough miracles in my life to believe this was one of them. I'm not sure why I was chosen. That's not up to me to know. However, I'm grateful for it. If it was part of the big plan to meet this young woman – who was sent by a friend to assist me in recovery – well, then I'd do it all over again."

"Ahh…" Abe sighed.

"Maybe," William added with a wink.

"Oh, and as far as the reward money goes," Ford said, "I have a confession to make. I'm the one who started the Find Our Guy Fund. I wanted help in finding you because… Well, because I wanted to find out what you just told me. I had to sneak away from home. I do feel bad about upsetting my mother, but she'll get over it. I think I know what I want to do with the money that came in, though."

"Yes?" William and Abe asked, now side by side, holding onto each other.

"I think I'll start a foundation for skate parks for kids. You know, get them started with small-wheeled stuff until they're older and can race cars and motorcycles. Bicycles, skateboards, roller skates, scooters – they can all share the same course. What's in that crowdfunding account isn't enough to get more than a few started, but I've been looking for a project. I think heading up a 'Wheels for Youth Foundation' might be a good start on using some of my inheritance."

"So, you *are* the missing Worthington heir, then," William said.

"Huh?" Abe asked.

"You really ought to watch television more, or at least listen to the news, Abe." William chuckled. "Then again, if you did, you might not have treated me the same way when you met me."

"Don't count on it. I don't trust anyone at first sight." She looked at Ford's disheveled appearance and swollen face. "Appearances can be deceiving."

Chapter 12

Joe Patterson, producer of Around the World in Eighty Cars, admitted that he was the one who submitted the doctored video that showed an extraterrestrial lifting the show's star, William Gagnant, from the burning Mustang in last month's spectacular explosion. "If you look closely at the face, you'll see the computer-generated creature is winking at the joke. It was all done in good fun. All proceeds from advertising on the post are being donated to For the Greater Good Burn Clinic. No aliens were harmed in the production of this video."

***

Abe snuggled close to William in front of her spacious living room window. Every scented candle she could find was burning. Plus, she had a pan of simmering apple juice with cinnamon sticks and cloves on the stove. "Didn't I tell you the view was magnificent?"

"I have to admit it's even more majestic than the one from *my* home."

"I think it's because we're on the second story. We can see further and wider because of the higher altitude. Now I know why Montana is called the Big Sky Country."

"Beautiful view and it smells better in here, too," William said, then kissed her on the temple.

"That's because of the boiling spices and candles."

William snuggled in closer, rubbing his nose in the hair behind her ear. "No, it's not. At least, that's not what I was talking about."

She giggled and leaned into him, briefly setting him off balance. She quickly caught him around the waist and helped him find his feet again. Embarrassed at making him falter and humbled by his words, she changed the subject. She'd been curious about the miracle rescue since she'd first heard about it. "An angel, huh?"

"Had to be." He turned to face her, so she'd have to look at him.

"*You* weren't in my life to save me from harm back then."

She looked down, hiding her blush, and felt a gentle hand on her chin, urging her to look at him. "Thank you for sticking around, even if I am an old fart." He kissed her gently then pulled away, making sure he hadn't been too forward.

"Well, not that old," she replied. "At least, not too old to learn how to kiss a woman properly. But before we get started, let's sit down and take a load off."

"I've been holding back but still, I'll let you 'learn me.' Beating up bad guys and filing police reports takes a lot out of a person."

William led her to the couch. He saw her backpack sitting by the bedroom door and let go of her hand as she sat down, making a detour.

"What's in this that knocked Razor for such a loop?" He lifted it by the strap. "It's not that heavy. It looked like there was an anvil in it when you hit him."

Abe bolted from the couch, trying to get the bag away from him before he looked inside. He held it away from her playfully. "Is there something in here you don't want me to see?"

She grabbed for it again, but he'd seen her intent and held it behind him.

"No," she said. She shrugged, pretending it didn't make a difference whether he looked in the bag or not.

He unzipped it but held her eye, not looking inside. "Maybe there's something in here that *you* don't want to see."

"Oh, sweet, sweet William. You challenge me. You haven't even known me a week and…" She grabbed for it again and this time, knocked it out of his hands. Sundry items from her last-minute packing that she hadn't put away spilled across her bedroom floor.

"What's this?" William asked, grasping the tank top-covered Titan, her battery-powered 'boyfriend.'

"Well, if you don't know, I'm not going to tell you."

William peeled the cotton shirt away, holding it at arm's length as if it was poisonous and might bite him. "Oh! Oh, my. A blue artificial…member? It looks like your American versions are quite a bit smaller. It must be the men they use for models, then. I'm sure you can do better with the equipment of a genuine boyfriend."

"What? Are you volunteering as a replacement?"

"Well, I am from 'Great' Britain, after all." He raised his eyebrows mischievously. "And I don't require batteries."

***

Pepé scampered across the ground, then stopped and sat up on his haunches, looking back at the big place he'd just left.

He'd had a comfortable bed there, and not having to scavenge for food was great. But then that one big man showed up, stomping on him for no reason. It was a dangerous place now. He'd stay away so he didn't have to defend himself again.

He'd miss his pet person, the one who fed him fruit and smelled so good. Yes, he'd miss her, but there was a different kind of scent in the air tonight, calling him. The aroma of females of his own kind was on the wind. He was stronger now. It was time for him to claim a mate and a hunting territory.

But he just might come back to the lady with sweet-smelling fingers someday and see if she had more apples.

And bring his new wife and kids.

(The end of the story…for now)

Afterword

Thank you for reading THE PUREBRED AND THE MUTT. Writing this story was a blast! If you had half as much fun reading it as I did creating it, then it's a success.

If you could take a moment to leave an honest review on the site where you purchased it, I'd appreciate it. Authors love even short reviews about what their readers liked about their stories.

My website (www.danihaviland.com) has my books and box sets listed with descriptions and links of where to purchase them. A few ebooks are even FREE! You can also sign up for my newsletter there.

Other Books from the Author

I have written *dozens* of books. Rather than list them all here, check out info on the major series of my Universe at **www.danihaviland.com**. There are also quite a few Stand-Alone singles available.

THE FAIRIES SAGA (historical fiction and time travel romance) is where it all began. I suggest starting this series with AYE, I AM A FAIRY.

ARLIE UNDERCOVER (romantic suspense with LGBTQ leads in the later books). From Alaska to Arizona and back again, Arlie is finding friends and a new family along the way while thwarting bad guys and protecting the good ones.

TRIPLETS: THREE AREN'T ONE (mixed genres including women's fiction and romantic comedy with LGBTQ leads) Grace was told her babies had died., so tried to get on with her life. What started as tragedy winds up one of the best Happy Ever Afters possible for everyone involved.

THAT TWIN THING (romantic suspense) The midwife took the unwanted twin to bring up as her own. Years later, the two young men meet under strained situations, neither one of them knowing the other existed. Redemption, forgiveness, and happy ever afters with a few surprises.

About the Author

USA Today Bestselling Author

 From crime thrillers to historical fantasy, two-hour quick reads to epic sagas, there's always an element of comedy in *USA Today Bestselling Author* Dani Haviland's stories. Her books and box sets have ranked in the top ten sellers in dozens of categories. Dani is also the owner of Chill Out! Books, publisher of scores of single titles and box sets.

Read them all and enjoy the diversity!

Contact information:

www.danihaviland.com

Email: dani@danihaviland.com

Twitter: @dani_haviland

Facebook: www.facebook.com/ChillOutDani

BookBub: https://www.bookbub.com/authors/dani-haviland

www.ingramcontent.com/pod-product-compliance
Lightning Source LLC
Chambersburg PA
CBHW070937250626
47159CB00009B/3292